SPY HIGH:
MISSION FIVE

B L O O D
RELATIONS

A. J. BUTCHER

LITTLE, BROWN AND COMPANY
New York ꞏ Boston

Little, Brown and Company

Time Warner Book Group
1271 Avenue of the Americas, New York, NY 10020
Visit our Web site at www.lb-teens.com

First U.S. Edition: April 2005
First published in Great Britain in 2003 by Atom Books

Cover art by Jason Reed

ISBN 0-316-78092-8 (pb)

10   9   8   7   6   5   4   3   2   1

Q-FF

Printed in the United States of America

PART ONE

CHAPTER ONE

Sometimes, Ben wondered whether the whole thing hadn't been a dream. It was all too perfect in his mind, every detail, every word, like an episode in a novel he had written himself, or a scene from a movie he'd watched a thousand times. Everything else that had happened to him at six years old he could scarcely now remember, but the day on the cliff top was one he would never forget.

Uncle Alex took him there, away from the party, the piercing jabber of excited children. Ben was glad to go. He didn't know who half of the children were anyway, and his parents had apparently invited the entire six-year-old population of Rhode Island to his birthday as a point of principle, and now that they'd offered their presents to him, like the Wise Men to the Baby Jesus, he was no longer interested. Besides, he'd have gone anywhere with Uncle Alex at any time. Ben adored Uncle Alex.

His uncle strode alongside him like a giant, like a statue of a hero come to life, leading him across the grounds to the cliff. Ben could already hear the crashing of the waves against the rocks, as if the sea was applauding him for being a Stanton and destined for great things, as everyone had always told him. He almost had to run to keep up.

At the cliff's edge they stopped, where the land seemed to have been torn away like a piece of paper. The ocean was a long way down to a young boy's eyes.

"I thought it was time we had a talk," said Uncle Alex, smiling at him and ruffling his blond hair.

"Yes, Uncle Alex," Ben replied obediently. It always made him feel special when his uncle chose to speak to him, singled out and privileged. He gazed up at the wise, handsome features, the hair prematurely flecked with dignified gray, the eyes that blazed blue and never seemed to blink, the wide and generous smile. When he grew up, he wanted to be just like Uncle Alex.

"What do you see, Ben?" The man pointed out beyond the headland. "Tell me what you see."

Ben's lower lip quivered. He couldn't see anything. It seemed to him that Uncle Alex's finger was pointing nowhere. But he had to give the right answer, had to. He couldn't let Uncle Alex down, not now that he was six. But he couldn't lie, either. "I don't . . . I don't . . ."

"The sky, Ben," said Uncle Alex gently. "You see the sky, don't you?" Ben nodded eagerly. Of course he saw the sky. "Good. Very good. And do you know what the sky stands for, Ben?"

This question seemed impenetrable to Ben, but he was going to hazard a guess at "daytime" before Uncle Alex supplied his own answer, almost as if he'd never expected Ben to try in the first place.

"It stands for dreams," he said. "It stands for ambition. Do you know what ambition is, Ben?"

"Something you've always wanted to do." He knew that one all right, the words tumbling out and almost tripping over one another in their haste.

"Good boy," Uncle Alex approved, and Ben flushed proudly. "And ambition is very important. Everyone has to have an ambition, a desire, something to give their lives meaning. Everyone needs to reach out to touch the sky. That's what I've brought

4

you here to tell you, Ben. I think you're old enough to know on your birthday. You must have ambitions, too."

"Yes, Uncle Alex." *As many as you want*, Ben thought.

"Because we are special people, Ben, your family, mine, others like us. You'll come to understand that as you grow older. We have been chosen to be great. We have been born to lead. What we own and what we are mean that there is nothing we cannot accomplish in our lives, nothing we cannot achieve." Ben felt a strange excitement in him that was also almost like tears. Uncle Alex filled his vision like the world. "But we have to have courage. We have to have strength. We have to believe in ourselves."

"Yes, Uncle Alex." Courage. Strength. Belief.

"Because if we do . . . what is there between us and the sky, Ben?"

"Nothing, Uncle Alex."

"Excellent. Excellent indeed. Nothing," the man repeated.

And he jumped off the cliff.

Ben blinked. His jaw worked. His body jerked back in sudden startlement. But he didn't scream or shout out or rush to the cliff's edge or cry for help. His brain simply could not process the information his eyes had transmitted to it. His mind couldn't register the fact that, for no apparent reason, Uncle Alex had leaped to certain death.

And then he didn't have to. Because then it wasn't true.

Uncle Alex rose again, and he was walking on air and he was laughing as if at some enormous joke. In the sky there were invisible stairs, and Uncle Alex was climbing them. He hadn't fallen. He couldn't fall. He could only go higher, scaling the sky until he stood above the earth like a god.

Ben tried to reach for him, but he was too far away, unattainable. And then something seized Ben's heart and misted his eyes, and he hung his head at six years old because he knew he'd never be able to live up to Uncle Alex's example. He'd never be like him, and he could spend his whole live striving.

Above and beyond, a man was throwing his arms wide with triumph.

"You see!" His voice boomed like thunder. "Nothing can stand in our way. Nothing!" And there was no one to contradict him.

"So, Ben, is that a harpoon gun in your wet suit or are you just pleased to see me?"

The leader of Bond Team regarded Bex Deveraux distastefully as she joined him on the side of the tank. "You trying to be funny?"

"Actually, yes. Problem?"

"Yeah. Don't bother. As a comedienne, you make a passable trainee secret agent." He tried to ignore Bex's jabbingly spiky hair, this week dyed purple, and the piercings in her nose and ears that even in a good mood he tended to interpret as a personal affront. And today, Benjamin T. Stanton Jr. was in anything but a good mood. "Why don't you just try and concentrate for once? This is supposed to be a lesson."

"Yes, sir, boss." Bex bobbed up and down in mock humility. "Whatever you say. Little Bex is gonna be a real good girl from now on."

With a derisive snort, Ben turned away and looked back across the shimmering surface of the tank, its deep waters crystal clear. *Concentrate.* Right now, he needed to take his own advice. Let Bex play the joker if she wanted — it must come from hanging around with Eddie too long. He'd focus on the targets in the far wall and the likely configuration of the light bars between him and them. He wouldn't even be distracted by the appearance of the remainder of his teammates.

"I feel like a penguin in these things." Eddie was bemoaning the necessity of wearing flippers. "And I'm sure this scuba gear's gonna give me a rash. How are you at applying ointment, Bex?"

"How are you at coping with disappointment, Eddie?"

Eddie adjusted the oxygen tank on his back and tightened the strap. "Suppose I can survive the discomfort for a bit," he admitted. "Could be worth it. Got to say, you girls could do wet suits for Armani, couldn't they, Jake? And I mean that in a caring way."

Cally shook her head pityingly. "Eddie, you are such a sleaze. And don't drag Jake into it. He respects us for our abilities, not just our looks, isn't that right, Jake?"

"Absolutely," Jake stressed. He waved his laser harpoon at Eddie. "This guy has nothing to do with me." Though the way his dark eyes lingered on Lori, cautiously, nervously, and retreated again as soon as she noticed, suggested he wasn't quite telling the truth, the whole truth, and nothing but the truth. Jake suddenly found his belt required attention.

Lori approached her boyfriend by the tank's edge. "Are you all right, Ben?"

"Shouldn't I be?" He'd snapped before he'd realized it, which rather suggested not. "Ouch. Sorry, Lo."

"You want me to try it again?"

"No, it's okay." A fake laugh. "A little tired, that's all. Got stuff on my mind. You know. My birthday and everything. Hanging around here, just want to get on with it."

"You've been working too hard," said Lori. "You've got to learn to relax sometime."

"Yeah," said Ben. "Sometime."

"Not right now though, huh?" Lori indicated the changing rooms.

Weapons Instructor Lacey Bannon had arrived to take the lesson.

"In a wet suit," Eddie sighed. "There is a God."

The teacher called Bond Team to order. Bannon was an expert with every device that could destroy, demolish, or otherwise do damage on the market, as well as most of them that weren't. Not necessarily a talent that would be looked for on the résumés of many members of staff at elite educational establishments, certainly, but Deveraux Academy was not a normal school. It looked like it from the outside, perhaps. To the untrained eye, the eye that saw no farther than the gothic buildings and the sports fields and the silent students who trooped neatly between lessons, the institution probably looked rather old-fashioned, if anything, straitlaced and as traditional as mortarboards and cold showers. But very few people saw beyond the school's illusory façade, very few got close enough to realize that the youngsters who formed the public face of Deveraux Academy were only holograms, and that its real flesh-and-blood students tended to spend their time several stories below ground, and on subjects in which it was not usual to take public examinations. At Spy High, English, math, and science rubbed shoulders with spycraft, surveillance, and shadowing techniques, and, in this instance, underwater espionage. Hence the scuba gear and laser harpoon guns: The tank was designed for more than just swimming.

Lacey spoke and the members of Bond Team listened. They hadn't reached the final term of their second and final year without learning when joking was appropriate and when it was not (although Eddie sometimes still needed reminding). "On missions that require you to go deep underwater," Lacey was reminding them, "your survival will depend on quickness of body, quickness of mind. Today's opening exercise will test both. To the limit."

"I don't like the sound of that," Eddie mumbled to Ben, his confidant for the moment by virtue of proximity. "If God had meant for us to flap about underwater, he'd have given us gills."

"I wish he'd given you a gag," muttered Ben.

"Is there a problem, Mr. Stanton, Mr. Nelligan?" Lacey's hearing was as sharp as her weaponry skills.

"No, Ms. Bannon," Ben said, coloring embarrassedly. "Nothing at all."

"I'm pleased to hear it. Then perhaps the two of you might like to go first, show the others how it's done."

"Of course, Ms. Bannon." Though Ben did not perhaps sound quite his usual, effortlessly arrogant self, at least he didn't to Lori. A faint frown smudged her forehead.

"If I kind of get into trouble, though, Ms. Bannon," said Eddie, "will you do the right thing and jump in and save me?"

"Nelligan," Lacey Bannon said, narrowing her eyes, "you don't want to know. Now masks on, fix your breathing apparatus, and let's get you underwater. I'm shutting the ceiling."

Ben and Eddie fitted their breathing tubes and dutifully slipped into the water, keeping a safe grip on their laser harpoons. Already the tank's reinforced Plexiglass cover was sliding into place, sealing them beneath the surface, making the environment within the vast rectangular receptacle their entire world. Ben allowed himself to sink to the very bottom of the tank, some dozen meters deep. He forced his eyes to adjust to the occasionally distorted tricks of the refracted light. He couldn't afford to make mistakes down here, not with the others watching.

"Bobbing along, bobbing along on the bottom of . . ." Eddie didn't seem to be having the same worries. His tuneless singing rang all too clearly in Ben's earpiece.

Lacey's voice brought it to a merciful end. "Into your starting positions," she instructed. "There is a competitive element to this, of course." *Of course*, Ben thought. His whole life was a competition. "Once I activate the light bars, you have five seconds to assimilate their position before the buzzer will sound for you to begin. Any contact between you and a light bar will result in a time penalty. Same thing if you're struck by a solar torpedo, which will be fired randomly after the buzzer. As soon as you get into the shoot zone, you can fire your harpoons but make it good. You get only once chance."

"Eddie 'Dead-Eye' Nelligan only needs one chance," boasted Eddie, brandishing his harpoon gun like he was about to let one fly at once.

Ben said nothing.

"I take it that means you're ready," said Lacey. "In that case, light bars on."

Immediately, horizontal poles of yellow light crisscrossed the tank, obstacles for the students to negotiate. Water swirled within them as in a tube. It was fifty meters to the shoot zone, but there was absolutely no possibility of reaching it in a straight line. You had to be virtually double-jointed to avoid the light bars, Ben knew from previous experience, and that was without also having to take evasive action to keep clear of the solar torpedoes. You needed to be functioning at the very peak of your powers to make a decent score in the tank. Maybe he wasn't sure about that, but he still ought to have enough left to give Eddie a good beating.

The buzzer sounded.

Ben powerfully propelled himself away from the wall, thrusting through the water, his arms by his sides, keeping his body as slim and streamlined as possible, like a harpoon itself. He arched up and over the first light bar, plunged down again with a kick of his flippers to sweep under the second, then forced his limbs into another abrupt change of direction. The water foamed around him, obscuring his vision through the mask, but he knew he'd accrued no penalty points yet and Eddie had to be behind him. Ben glanced to his left to make certain.

Concentrate.

From the right, as if waiting for its chance, the white flash of a solar torpedo. He had to move. Fast. Ben wheeled in the water, crooked and curved his body, saw the danger stab uselessly past him and evaporate against the floor of the tank. But there was no time for self-congratulation. His momentum had been disrupted and the light bars seemed to be closing in like a cell, and Eddie was ahead of him and swimming like he knew what he was doing.

Ben strove to catch up. His legs were strong. His body obeyed. He darted between the light bars, accelerating again, needing only to arch from one side to the other to avoid more solar torpedoes. The shoot zone was ahead. He and Eddie were neck and neck. He swung his harpoon gun into play. Just one more light bar to negotiate. Just one. Directly in his path.

Flip up. Flip down. Didn't matter. Wouldn't make a difference. Easy maneuver either way. Just go either way. Fifty-fifty.

And Ben hesitated. Kind of went down but kind of went up as well. His thigh brushed the bar, was faintly smeared with yellow, like a spill of paint. Just a little and just for a second. But in the espionage business, little and seconds meant life and death.

Penalty points.

Ben cursed himself for his stupidity, reached the shoot zone, and fired his laser harpoon. The bolt missed the bull's-eye by a fraction.

Nelligan's had hit dead center.

Eddie was still celebrating after they'd showered, changed, and retired to the rec room for a Coke. "I thank you. I thank you." Graciously acknowledging an array of imaginary fans. "Dead-Eye Nelligan strikes again. Didn't I tell you they used to call me Dead-Eye Nelligan?"

"Among other things, I'm sure," smirked Cally.

"And Eddie, are you going to sit down or are you going to parade around in circles with your hands in the air all day?" Jake grumbled. "You're making me nervous."

"Sorry, Jake," Eddie said, not sounding like it, "but it's not often I beat our fearless leader at anything. I've got to make the most of it, right?"

"Don't be stupid, Eddie," scolded Lori. The others had found Eddie's victory over Ben pretty funny, largely because it had been so surprising, but she didn't. She knew that Ben hated to lose at anything to anyone, and that to do so was never a laughing matter. His expression ought to have told his teammates the same thing. Ben sat now, stooped and glowering over his drink, and he'd said scarcely anything since Lacey's lesson.

"Well, I don't know," Eddie continued to brag. "On the other hand, maybe this is a turning point, the first of many triumphs. What do you think, Ben? Maybe I'm just a late developer."

"I think you better shut up," Ben warned with menace in his voice, "before I shut you up."

"Hey, Ben, there's no need for that," Bex protested.

"What's the matter with you, Stanton?" Jake couldn't resist a jibe for old time's sake. "Finding it hard to cope with the fact that you're human like the rest of us?"

"Jake." Lori sounded hurt.

"No, I think I'm on a roll now," pursued Eddie. "I think you're gonna see me on top of everything before too long, I can feel it coming. In fact, is there anything in the school rules about re-electing team leaders in the final term? 'Cause I'd just like to put myself forward if anyone feels —"

Ben was on his feet. "I told you!" He was seizing Eddie's collar. "To shut up!" And there was violence in his glare.

The others rose, too, suddenly concerned. Students glanced across the rec room with interest to where Bond Team was causing a disturbance again.

"Ben, don't!" cried Lori. She saw his clenched fists.

Eddie gulped. He saw them, too, and a blue rage in Ben's eyes. "Only joking, Ben. Honest . . ."

Ben seemed suddenly aware of his teammates surrounding him, regarding him with a mixture of caution, curiosity, and confusion. He couldn't stay there while they were looking at him like that. "Out of my way." He pushed Eddie aside and stalked out of the rec room. The others watched him go in bewilderment.

IGC Data Monitor Subsection: Cults
Key: The Temple of the Transformation
And the herald of the Lord came to him in a dream and said: "Awake, Calvin Johns, for you have slept too long. Rise up and do the Lord's bidding."

And the man who was Calvin Johns did as the herald bade him to do, though in his heart he was so afraid, and he said: "I am the Lord's true and humble servant. Teach me his will."

And the herald of the Lord spoke words as pure as fire: "The world has fallen into sin and iniquity, and a black cloud of evil is upon the earth and the knowledge of the Lord has withered away like rotten fruit on a dying tree. The time has come for a new beginning and a new belonging. The time has come for the Transformation. And nothing will ever be the same again."

Then Calvin Johns stood truly in the presence of the herald of the Lord, and the herald placed his hands upon him and his former flesh fell away like winter clothing on a summer's day, and he stood a man reborn.

"Your old life is dead," the herald told him. "Your old name is lost. You are Gabriel, Chosen of the Lord, and you will lead His people to the glorious Transformation He has promised all those of faith. Turn your back on all you have known and follow me."

And Gabriel did, and he never walked again the ways of his youth. He trod in the footsteps of the herald of the Lord, and he left the city behind him and the clamor and the chaos of men. He walked into the wilderness, not stopping once for sleep or earthly sustenance, strong in faith and living in the Lord. He walked until his feet bled scarlet, but he felt no pain.

At last, the herald raised his hand and in a desert made by man they paused, beneath a sky thick with fumes and the soil desolate and scarred, where nothing good could grow and hope seemed gone.

And the herald said: "This is the place. In this forsaken wasteland the change will come. You, Gabriel, will bring life back to this barren earth and in this place build a Temple to the Lord the likes of which has never been seen. From the very ashes of destruction will rise the Temple of the Transformation, and its light will cover all the world."

And Gabriel said: "Let it be so."

Lori found him at the laser range. It didn't exactly come as a shock. Miss a bull's-eye by a width of a harpoon and spend the next three days in sackcloth and ashes paying a kind of marksman's penance, that was Ben's way. Lori supposed she should be used to it by now.

If he observed her entry, he didn't show it, just kept on firing at the target — bull's-eye after bull's-eye. None of them counted, of course, because none of them had come when it mattered.

"Ben," she called above the electric zap of the laser, "you know you can stop whenever you want, don't you?"

"Lori? What are you doing here?" His tone wasn't exactly hostile, but not exactly let-me-take-you-in-my-arms-and-show-you-how-much-I-care, either.

"At this time of night, I was about to ask you the same question. Doesn't the fact that the place is as empty as Eddie's brain tell you something?"

"I've got to practice, Lo." *Zap.* Bull's-eye. "I got sloppy today." *Zap.* Bull's-eye. "I can't let that happen again." He took aim once more but this time didn't fire his laser pistol. Lori's hand rested on his arm, gently lowered it. "What do you think you're doing?"

"Calling time out, William Tell," she said. "We need to talk."

"Right now? About what?" Ben didn't catch her eye, like

someone with a guilty secret. "What if you leave me a note or something? You know, and I'll get back to you in the morning."

"This won't wait until the morning. I need to know now."

"Well?" Still evasive, uncomfortable.

Lori fixed her own blue eyes on him. Ben could never normally resist them. "What's going on?"

"What do you mean, what's going on? What's going on is I'm doing some nice quiet laser practice, which I'd very much like to get back to —"

"Ben." Lori's tone hardened.

He sighed. "Nothing. Nothing's going on."

"This is Spy High, Ben. We're training to be spies, remember? That means we're trained to notice things, and I'd have to be the most shortsighted student in the history of the school not to notice that something is worrying you. Something is on your mind and it's obviously not good. This business with Eddie today, that's just a symptom. Tell me what's really wrong."

Ben's gaze flickered cautiously to hers. He tried a reassuring smile. "It's nothing, Lori. Honestly. I'm just a bit stressed, that's all. Like you said — been working too hard. Guess we're all under pressure with finals at the end of term."

Lori shook her head, unconvinced. "You've always thrived under pressure, Ben. There's more to it than that. Why won't you tell me? I'm your girlfriend. We've been together for over a year. That gives me confiding rights if you didn't know, it's in the Girlfriend's Charter, and I'm not allowed to take no for an answer." She smiled encouragingly. "Come on. Trust me. Talk to me. I want to help."

And there was a moment then when it looked like she'd won, when it seemed that Ben was on the brink of opening up and telling her the truth, but at the final second, the Stanton shutters came down again, as on a house that none were permitted to enter. "That's good, Lori," he said. "I'm pleased. But there's nothing to help me with, nothing I can't work out for myself. Really."

Lori frowned, felt her failure sharply. It felt like rejection. "All right, Ben, if that's the way you want it. Nothing you can't work out for yourself. Guess you don't need me around then, do you?" Offering him another chance.

"I just want to shoot a few more of these." He was already returning his attention to the range. "Maybe I'll see you in the rec room later, okay?"

"Okay," said Lori. "Maybe."

Zap. Bull's-eye. She watched him for a while. *Zap.* Bull's-eye. She watched him thoughtfully. *Zap.* Bull's-eye.

But when he turned to look for her, she was gone.

The streets didn't frighten Mac Luther. To some, they were dangerous, threatening, a dark labyrinth where the rejects of society wandered like ghosts, where junkies and muggers and worse skulked and lurked. To some, the streets in this crippled part of town were to be avoided at all costs, particularly after nightfall. But to Mac Luther, these streets were home. He'd been born here. He belonged here. And he'd spent the past thirty years of his adult life trying to make a difference here.

Everyone knew him, his features as weathered and battered as a retired boxer's. Everyone knew the Refuge, the shelter he'd established a decade before to offer hope, security, and a full belly to the homeless young people and runaways who might otherwise be forced into crime out of despair. Mac was a familiar figure roaming the streets at all hours, constantly on the lookout for those in need of help. He didn't care where he went or when. The streets didn't frighten him.

Only lately, even Mac had grown uneasy. Something was happening, something was changing, and he didn't like it. There was a new influence on the streets now, one that could be summed up in five words: the Temple of the Transformation.

At first, he'd tried to convince himself that he was worrying over nothing. If he'd had a dollar for every religious cult that had tried to stake a claim in the hearts and minds of the neighborhood over his lifetime, he'd have been able to rebuild the entire area himself. They came and went like the seasons. And, to be fair (which Mac found he could be only grudgingly in this case), the Temple's message seemed essentially positive, that inside themselves everyone had the power to transform their lives and make themselves new. It wasn't the Temple's teaching that bothered him. It was its teachers.

They called themselves "disciples," and they wore robes as black as if they'd been cut from the night itself. They patrolled the streets relentlessly, almost more than he did, but never alone like Mac, always in groups (or gangs, he sometimes thought, uncharitably). And they were highly proactive in their search for recruits. Mac had heard tales from kids at the Refuge, of disciples almost physically seizing homeless youngsters and whisking them off to the great church they'd built on the site of a slum not far away. Mac didn't know how true that was, but he did know that over the past month or so, he'd seen clutches of Temple disciples hanging around outside the Refuge, trying to engage his charges in conversation, and that he'd felt compelled on more than one occasion to ask them to move on. They had done so, Mac sensed, but with increasing reluctance, like they felt they were a force whose time was coming.

And now this. The hoverport, where buses brought strays from all over the country, hoping to find their fortune in the city. Tonight, the disciples of the Temple of the Transformation had found *them*. Mac saw the two girls, barely teenagers, it seemed, a paltry bag of belongings at their feet, standing together half-defensively and half-defiantly as five figures in dark robes encircled them like a trap. Three men. Two women. All smiling fixed and false.

"You'll be safe with us." Mac could hear the words, soothing and hypnotic. "Come with us. The Temple will look after you."

"There's nothing for you to worry about, nothing at all. There's a hot meal and a warm bed waiting for you both."

The girls shunned the offer, seemed eager to move on. "We don't have to go with you," said one.

"Yeah, get lost," said the other, with a courage she didn't necessarily feel. "Just go and leave us alone."

"What are you talking about? Don't be foolish. You're alone here. We can help. Come with us. You know you want to. . . ."

"I don't think they do." Mac's voice was firm and confident. The disciples turned in interest toward him. "So maybe you'd better do as they ask and leave them alone."

"And what business is this of yours, old man?" said the central disciple coolly. His four companions fanned out to either side. They could surround him if they wanted to. The moved toward him like they might.

Mac stood his ground. "The welfare of children is everyone's business," he said. "You girls, I run a shelter not far from here. If you want somewhere to stay for the night, you can stay there. No strings."

"Of course." The central disciple's smile seemed to expand as it became even less real. "I know who you are. Luther. The Uncle Remus of the runaways. Well, I'm afraid your Refuge has had its day, old man."

"Is that right?" It occurred to Mac that the disciples might actually attack him. *Well, they'd get a shock if they did.*

"Oh, yes. You see, these streets belong to us now, to the Temple. We have accepted the responsibility of bringing the glories of Transformation to the people, and we will allow no one to stand in the way of our holy mission."

"And what if people don't want the *glories* of Transformation?" said Mac.

"They will, when there's nowhere else for them to go."

"Is that a threat?"

"May the blessing of Gabriel the Chosen be upon you —" the disciple smiled by way of response "— old man."

With the slightest of gestures to his companions, the disciple led the way past Mac and beyond. The five of them seemed to melt into the night. Permanently, Mac hoped, though he doubted the presence of the Temple could be wished away as easily as that. One thing was certain, however. It would be wise for him to find out a little more about the Temple of the Transformation and its plans. And then he'd think about contacting Spy High.

CHAPTER TWO

Eddie leaned back in the hoverlimo's plush seat and luxuriated. "This is the life, isn't it?" he said. "Sure beats Ethics in Espionage last thing on a Friday afternoon."

"Removing one's toenails with a pair of rusty tweezers beats Ethics in Espionage last thing on a Friday afternoon," remarked Bex, reclining alongside him. "Theoretically, of course," she added quickly. "Just in case you were wondering."

"I suppose we should be grateful to Ben for supplying such a select form of transport." Cally indicated the chauffeur, the final uniformed touch to the splendor of the limo.

Jake grunted skeptically. "Yeah, well, Stanton's never gonna miss a chance to impress us, is he? Not even in his absence." He opened the minibar that was set into the side of the limo and selected a Coke and a root beer.

"I didn't know you liked root beer, Jake," said Cally.

"I don't —" Jake winked "— but I'm sure as Stanton's loaded I'm going to get my money's worth out of this trip. Drink, anyone?"

"Actually, I think we owe a vote of thanks to your dad, too, Bex," said Eddie, reaching for a glass and a Coke. "I mean, if he hadn't given permission for a weekend pass, Ben's sixteenth would be down four VIP guests and we wouldn't be sipping drinks in a car the size of most people's living rooms. For a computer program, Mr. D. is still an okay guy in my book."

"Well, I'm sure Dad would be pleased to hear you say so, Eddie," acknowledged Bex graciously, "though I brought some of my own influence to bear as well. It's no good being the founder's daughter if you can't take advantage of your position once in a while."

Eddie leered across at her. "Speaking of taking advantage of your position . . ."

"Yeah?" Bex smiled innocently, dabbed at the recliner control on Eddie's seat. With a cry of surprise, he was thrown flat on his back, Coke splattering over his face. "What's the matter, Eddie? Can't hold your drink?"

"No fair, Bex. Look, this is gonna stain the fabric now. What are we going to tell Ben? We've ruined his limo."

"I shouldn't worry, Ed," Jake said. "I expect they've got another."

"Wonder how Lori's getting on," mused Cally. She and Ben had been granted special permission from Jonathan Deveraux to leave school midweek to travel to Ben's home in Newport, Rhode Island, to prepare for his birthday celebrations. It was a privilege reserved only for the most special occasions. "I'm not sure she was entirely looking forward to meeting Ben's family."

"If they're all like him," chuckled Jake wickedly, "how could she be?"

"That's not fair, Jake," Cally reprimanded lightly. "Anyway, I suppose we'll find out soon enough."

The appearance of the rest of Bond Team couldn't come soon enough for Lori, not that she'd dare tell that to Ben. To be fair, at the start of her stay, everything had been fine. The Stanton house itself was a little overpowering, true: an aristocratic mansion set in sumptuous acres of land overlooking Rhode Island Sound, complete with its own jetty and tennis courts outside, while interior features included a swimming pool of Olympic proportions, a movie theater, and an art collection that made the Louvre look like a flea market. Lori's own family was not exactly claiming Welfare, but on this evidence the Stantons were wealthier than most small nations. It took a little bit of coming to terms with, but Lori tried, and she was helped by the fact that returning home had seemed to change Ben's mood for the better. He seemed as happy and outgoing as Lori had seen him in weeks. Maybe he *had* just been working too hard.

And to begin with, it wasn't too much of an ordeal making the acquaintance of Ben's parents, either, even if they did tend to inspect her as if she were an ornament they were considering purchasing for the mantelpiece, and even if Ben's mother in particular did have a habit of clasping her hands together, nodding her head approvingly and repeating, "Charming, charming." Benjamin and Nancy Stanton — "Call us Ben and Nancy," Benjamin Sr. had said, as if she'd planned to call them anything else.

But then it occurred to her that Ben's parents, from whom he'd obviously inherited the blond hair and blue eyes, looked just like she and Ben might in another thirty years. And *then* it occurred to her that they were regarding her thoughtfully, almost calculatingly, like they were planning ahead, like Ben's sixteenth might be a dry run for a rather more life-changing big day sometime in the future. And then more of Ben's relatives called, and there was even more cooing, complimenting, like it was visiting time at the mansion and the prize exhibit was Lori Angel. Perhaps they imagined she was enjoying being the center of attention. Only she wasn't. By the time Alexander Cain arrived, Lori was already more than halfway to feeling trapped.

"It's okay, Lo," Ben sympathized. "I know it's kind of like you've been on parade and everything, but you can't blame my relatives for wanting to look at you. If I was them, so would I.

Luckily, I get to see you a little more often." He squeezed her and kissed her.

"Ben," cautioned Lori, not altogether humorously, "be careful. Great-Aunt Petunia might be watching."

"Yeah, well, sorry if it's been a bit much. I can't help wanting to show you off. I'm really glad you're here, Lo."

An obvious line for her to reciprocate with a hearty "me, too." Lori got as far as a smile. Jake and the others would be near now. Friday evening was closing in.

"Anyway," Ben was continuing, "Uncle Alex isn't like the rest of my family. I've told you. You'll like him. Everybody likes him. Come on. If there's one person I wanted you to meet, it's Uncle Alex."

He certainly cut an imposing figure. Tall, handsome, dignifyingly graying as a man approaching fifty ought to be, he dominated even the richly furnished lounge where Lori was introduced. "Alexander Cain," he said, taking her hand. "I'm very pleased to meet you, Lori. Ben's said so much about you, and none of it does you justice."

"Thank you." Lori blushed. The man's eyes, as blue as Ben's but colder, somehow, like deep waters, made her feel self-conscious. "Alexander *Cain?*" *Not Stanton*, she was thinking.

"Uncle Alex isn't my real uncle," Ben admitted.

"You see, Lori," Alexander Cain's smile glittered, "I'm here under false pretenses. I'm only a friend of the family."

"There's no 'only' about it," declared Ben. "I've known Uncle Alex all my life, Lo. I hope he won't mind me saying it, but he's been as great an influence on me as anyone. I don't think I'd even *be* me if it wasn't for him."

Uncle Alex shrugged modestly. "Would you like something

to drink, Lori, or perhaps one of these canapés that the butler insists on leaving around? And then maybe you'd better tell me if you're the kind of girlfriend who likes to know all the embarrassing details of her boyfriend's younger years. I can tell you everything, free of charge."

Lori laughed. "Maybe you'd better leave that to Ben, Unc —"

"Alex," the man corrected smoothly. "No need for 'uncle.' Alex. And I'm sure Ben wouldn't object, would you, Ben?"

Lori laughed again, though not because Alexander Cain's gaze remained settled rather intrusively upon her, like a hand on her knee.

"Tell Lori about the time you jumped off the cliff out there," said Ben.

"Jumped off the what?" Lori gladly turned to Ben.

"Yeah," he grinned. "Uncle Alex was giving me advice about how you can do anything if you've got the courage, and then he just threw himself over the edge, and I'm thinking . . . well, I'm thinking the worst. And then before I can dare to peek over the cliff, he comes floating up in the sky again, completely unharmed. And I'm thinking, 'He can fly. Uncle Alex can do anything, he can even fly.' But of course, he wasn't actually flying."

"Airwalkers," Cain said. "Vital fashion accessory in the 2050s. 'You Too Can Walk on Air.' They helped to prove a point."

"I bet they must have," said Lori without enthusiasm.

"That was on my sixth birthday," Ben remembered. "Any surprises planned for my sixteenth, Uncle Alex?"

Alexander Cain smiled. "Oh, I'm sure I'll think of something. But right now, I'm eager to learn a little more about the charming Lori."

Even though he wasn't moving, Lori felt that somehow Cain

was advancing upon her, invading her personal space. "Oh, there's not really much to say," she retreated. "I'm not very interesting, really."

"I can't believe that."

"Well, I'm afraid it's true." *What had Ben said? Everybody liked his Uncle Alex?* Well, maybe she was the exception to the rule.

"I understand you attend Deveraux Academy with Ben," Cain prompted.

Lori nodded, wishing she was there now. Didn't Ben see anything wrong in the way Uncle Alex was scrutinizing her, like a man with a dirty magazine.

"Lo, you okay?"

"Excuse me, Master Ben . . ." Saved by the butler. "You asked me to let you know — your other classmates have arrived."

"Excellent!" Lori felt relief flooding through her. "Ben, quick, I can't wait to see them." She flicked a hurried glance at Cain. "Nice talking to you." *Even nicer rushing from the room.*

"Hold on a minute, Lo!" Ben called after her. "Did someone fire a starting gun?" He turned apologetically to Uncle Alex. "Sorry about that. Guess I'd better . . ." He gestured awkwardly after Lori. "She's kind of excitable."

"She's kind of delightful," said Alexander Cain. "You've chosen well, Ben."

"Do you think so?" Ben flushed proudly. "I mean, I think so, obviously."

"Lori's clearly very special. I look forward to getting to know her better." Alexander Cain smiled.

The party was well under way. So many lights blazed from the windows of the Stanton mansion that it looked as if the building was aflame, but even that was not illumination enough. Strings of brightly colored bulbs hung above the paths and between the trees nearest the house like an enchanted web, and beacon lamps burned all the way to the sound. The guests, most of whom could count the number of times they'd actually spoken to the lucky birthday boy on the thumbs of one hand, milled around eating and drinking as much as they could without being obvious about it. A band was playing on the lawn and another in a tent for the cake-cutting ceremony, the climax of the evening's formalities, which would take place at ten.

Bond Team, minus Ben, seemed to have reserved its place early.

"Is it me," wondered Eddie, "or does this tent have an echo? You could probably fit your dome inside it and still not touch the canvas, couldn't you, Jake?"

"Probably," Jake said, fidgeting with the knot of his tie. Ties and Jake Daly did not go together. If captured by the bad guys, Jake could doubtlessly endure tortures ranging from thumb screws to electric shock treatments without cracking, but force him to wear a tie and he'd be spilling Spy High secrets within minutes. He hoped Ben would appreciate the sacrifice, but doubted he'd notice. "Not quite the kind of people you'd see in a dome, though." He indicated their fellow guests.

"I know what you mean." Cally wrinkled her nose in distaste. Wealth and privilege emanated from the young people who surrounded them like an exotic perfume. "The only thing I have in common with these guys is four limbs and a head."

Bex noticed a group of boys who all seemed to have buck teeth and curly hair staring at her. She waved to them boldly. "Hi! How are you this evening? Yes, I'm pierced and I've got purple hair, but don't worry. It's not contagious." The boys turned away in quick embarrassment. Bex shook her head pityingly. "It's inbreeding that does it, you know," she observed to the others.

"Ben's parents didn't exactly seem big fans of the pierced and purple look, either," noted Eddie, "until they learned you were a Deveraux, of course. Then, somehow, hair color didn't seem to matter. Funny about that."

"The rich look after the rich," said Jake. Now his jacket seemed to be bothering him, tight about his powerful shoulders.

"Well, I think we ought to remember we're not here for any of these people," Lori gestured dismissively. "We're here to support Ben."

"Very loyal, Lo," grunted Jake. "So where is he, anyway? And why aren't you with him?"

"Oh —" she glanced toward the entrance of the tent "— he's probably talking with his Uncle Alex or something. Uncle Alex seems to take priority over just about everything."

"Is that jealousy I sense there, Lo?" teased Bex. "Got yourself a rival, have you?"

"That's very good, Bex. I'm amused." Lori shifted in her seat uncomfortably. "I mean, Alexander Cain is like Ben's mentor — you know how highly he thinks of him. But me, I just don't understand what Ben sees in him. He's a bit of a creep, if you ask me."

"Who?" Eddie asked guilelessly. "Ben or Cain?"

"Cain," Lori stressed with conviction. "So I'm trying to keep out of his way without hurting Ben's feelings."

"Looks like you might have blown it, Lo," said Cally. "Happy birthday to you, dum da dum dum dear Been . . ."

Ben himself was bearing down on them from the other side of the tent. He was smiling to the right and left but in a restless, impatient kind of way, like someone who was feeling almost too intensely the importance of the occasion, someone who was desperate for things to go right. The cost of his suit, Cally found herself thinking, could probably have kept an average family of four in food for a year, though he did look good in it.

"Lori, what do you think you're doing? I've been looking everywhere for you."

"Not quite everywhere," said Jake, earning a passing scowl.

"Is something wrong?" Lori felt on the defensive. "We've been right here."

"Don't tell me the caviar's run out already." Jake again.

"We've been having a good time, Ben," added Eddie. "Apparently, that's what you do at parties."

The way Ben was fixing his gaze on Lori suggested disagreement.

Bex grabbed hold of Eddie's tie and tugged it like a leash. "Well, let's go and do some more of it then, and give Ben and Lori some space. You can show me how badly you can dance." The two of them headed for the floor.

"Can we do close stuff or is it don't touch only?" Eddie left asking.

"And actually, Jake and I were about to go get another drink, weren't we?" Cally cued.

"Were we?" Jake seemed to have developed a sudden problem with his short-term memory.

"Yes, we were. Because you're very thirsty tonight."

"Parched," recalled Jake.

"So we'll see you both later. The cutting of the cake if not before." Cally grinned and flourished her forearm. "I've got my regulation Spy High bracelet camera right here."

"Well?" Ben pressed as soon as Cally and Jake were out of earshot.

"Well what?" Lori countered.

"What do you think you're doing?" Must have been a rhetorical question, as Lori was given no opportunity to reply. "You're supposed to be with me tonight, *seen* with me. It's my birthday party in case you've forgotten, and you're my girl."

"I know that."

"Then why aren't you acting like it?"

"Girl, yes. Shadow, not quite. I'm allowed to mingle, aren't I? Talk to our friends?"

"You can talk to them any time. There are people here tonight who've never met you before, people I want to introduce you to now. Can't do that if you're hiding away with Daly and the others."

"Hiding, Ben?" Lori looked pointedly around her at the swell of guests in the tent. "Well, if this is the best we can do, we sure aren't going to pass the camouflage and concealment test back at Spy High."

Ben was well practiced in ignoring sarcasm. "Besides," he pursued, "Uncle Alex says he wants to see you. . . ."

"Of course he does," Lori muttered, dismayed. But what if she didn't want to see him? Too late, as she observed Alexander Cain's undeniably impressive form entering the tent. Luckily, there was another way out as well. Lori kissed Ben lightly on the cheek. "Listen, you're going to have to excuse me a second. Urgent business."

"What?"

"Of the powdering-of-the-nose variety. Don't worry. I'll be back." *When Cain's gone,* she thought.

"Lori, wait." Ben sounded pained. "You can't just —"

But she could. And she did. And Jake watched her go from the bar. He watched Alexander Cain arrive, too, and Ben smiled sheepishly, apologetically. He watched and he wondered.

There were few people in the house, yet it still seemed full. The portraits of Stantons past gathered around her on the walls and peered down on Lori like judges, appraising and assessing her. Ridiculously, their cool blue gazes made her nervous, and she saw something of Ben in every one. If Ben Sr. and Nancy had their way, maybe one day she would join the dead in their gilt-edged frames and become a permanent fixture at the family home, immortalized in paint. The idea made her uncomfortable.

What was she doing here, roaming the rooms like a troubled spirit? There was no reason not to be with Ben. It was nearly ten and time for the cake to be cut. Time for her boyfriend to be cheered and applauded and she by his side. Lucky Ben Stanton: rich, talented, and with a gorgeous girl like Lori Angel at his disposal. Sixteen and his life ahead of him. The boy who had everything.

Lori frowned at the direction of her thoughts. Ben wasn't the only one in them now. If she was honest with herself, he hadn't been for a while, maybe not for a long while. The Stantons regarded her disapprovingly, their smiles stern. Maybe not since Jennifer's death, or even before that, when Simon Macey had duped her and somebody had helped her out. Somebody wild, dark, intense. Somebody who had suffered and survived.

She wondered what Jake was doing right now.

"Ah, here you are." A voice that oozed from the lips like oil spilling on a beach. Alexander Cain stood in the doorway like Samson between the pillars of the Temple. "Hello again, Lori. I have an idea that you've been avoiding me."

"Of course not." Lori tried for shocked innocence, noting that unlike the tent, there was only one entrance in this room. "Whatever made you think that?"

"Oh, I don't know." Cain held a drink in one hand. He shook it a little and ice cubes clinked. "Perhaps the fact that you're in here while everyone else is outside, including my protégé — your loving boyfriend."

Lori reddened. "Actually, I was just going to find Ben."

"Of course you were. I've no doubt you've been looking very hard for him." The smile slithered like a snake across Cain's face.

"I lost my way," defended Lori.

"I have another idea. It's that you don't seem to like me, Lori, and I'm just wondering why that might be."

"Well, it's not true." Lori wondered whether she could dart past him. "I hardly even know you." Probably not. "Now, I really ought to get back to Ben . . ."

"In time," permitted Alexander Cain, "because now seems a perfect opportunity for you to get to know me better. And vice versa, don't you think? Together as we are. Alone as we are." Cain stepped farther into the room. "What do you say?"

She didn't say anything. There was space opening up on either side of him. His right hand held the glass. She made her dash to his right.

Didn't make the door.

Alexander Cain simply dropped the glass — it shattered on the polished wooden floor — and stabbed out his arm, seizing

Lori's with surprising swiftness and strength. "Now that *is* rude," he observed, grasping her firmly.

"Let go of me!" Lori couldn't believe what was happening. "What do you think you're doing?"

"Getting to know you better." Cain's left hand took the liberty of fondling her long blonde hair. "Such beautiful hair. Ben must be proud."

Lori was on the brink of sending Alexander Cain the same way as his drink. Only the fact that this sleazebag was Ben's uncle made her pause. That was enough to make a difference.

"So is this a private party or can anyone join in?" Jake seemed mildly curious. "By the way, I'd take your hands off her if I were you, Mr. Cain, or the next time you visit your manicurist he or she won't be able to recognize them."

Alexander Cain laughed at that, but his grip relaxed sufficiently for Lori to tear herself free and join Jake by the door. "Jake," she said appreciatively. "That's what I call timing."

"Behold the knight, not in shining armor but a badly fitting suit," chuckled Cain. "What an indictment of our modern world." His sharp eyes narrowed to blades. "Though I think I can see why Ben is searching for you in vain, young Lori."

"I'll tell him what you've done," Lori snapped. "I'll tell him what his wonderful Uncle Alex is really like."

Alexander Cain seemed to find this the most amusing prospect of all. "You can try, sweet creature," he dared, "but he'll never believe you. He'll believe me. Ben will always believe me. Now, I think I need another drink. You will excuse, won't you?"

As Cain passed, Jake almost snatched at him, but Lori held his arm.

"Are you okay?" Concern and anger were equally etched on Jake's dark brow.

Lori nodded. "Just give me a minute. I didn't expect to have to fight off an advance from the revered Uncle Alex."

"The guy's a slimeball," Jake declared. "Rich guys, they think they can take what they want, do what they like. That's why the world's in such a mess."

"Yeah, thanks for the speech, Senator Daly."

"I could go on, but we'd better move. Ben's already scouring the place like a crime scene searching for you. That's why I'm here. There's a cake that needs to be cut, and you know how our noble leader's a stickler for punctuality. You ready?"

Lori smiled, realized she was still holding Jake's hand, and disentangled her fingers from his. "I'm a student at Spy High," she said. "I'm always ready."

They walked briskly back toward the mansion's main entrance. The music of the bands and the animated chatter of the guests drifted toward them like the promise of a better day.

"What are you going to do?" Jake asked. "About Cain?"

"What can I do? Keep out of his way, I suppose. Beyond tomorrow, I can't imagine I'll ever have to see him again."

"But you can't let him get away with it." Jake was indignant. "Pawing you like that." Lori knew that Jake was right. "Guys like that, you've got to let someone know. At the very least, you've got to tell Ben."

And then it happened, exactly what Lori didn't want to happen, and her evening plunged deeper into a nightmare. Who was the last person she wanted to see striding toward them just at this moment?

"Tell me what?" demanded Ben.

Lori closed her eyes, wished she was somewhere else, prefer-ably somewhere far away where there was time to think.

"Tell me what?" Anxiously, defensively. "And where have you *been*, Lori? If Uncle Alex hadn't just told me you were in here —" significant pause "— with Jake, I might never —"

"Cain told you?" Jake snorted.

"Mr. Cain to you, Daly," Ben retorted, "and if I was the least bit insecure, I might start wondering why you're inside with my girl while everyone else is outside enjoying the party."

Jake shook his head pityingly. "You've got the wrong guy, Stanton. You need to look closer to —"

"Jake!" Lori intervened. "No."

"No what?" Ben glanced suspiciously between them. "What's going on?"

His accusing tone struck a chord. Lori believed in the truth. "Go back to the others, Jake," she said quickly. "Ben and I will be out soon."

"Soon?" complained Ben, though glad to see the back of Daly. "It's got to be now. There's over a hundred people out there waiting for us to cut the cake."

"This is important, Ben, more important than 'Happy Birth-day to You.'"

"What?" She was serious. He could see it. A strange fear set-tled un-Stanton-like in his stomach. He began to wish he'd not asked. "Look, Lori, maybe we ought to —"

"It's Cain, Ben."

"Uncle Alex?" Now Ben was baffled. Distant music buzzed at his ears like wasps.

"He made a pass at me."

"He what?" From outside he could hear laughter. Someone

had cracked a good joke. "What are you talking about, Lo? Uncle Alex? That's impossible. You must have made some sort of mistake."

"I didn't. It happened." Lori spoke calmly but adamantly. "He came on to me in the lounge back there and if Jake hadn't —"

"Ah, Jake, Jake." Ben's expression turned crafty. "Now we're getting somewhere."

"No, we're not." Lori took both of Ben's hands in hers. "Alexander Cain isn't who you think he is. He tried to get it on with me, Ben. Don't you believe me?"

Their eyes locked. Lori's: passionate, pleading. Ben's: uncertain, denying. It was the moment she knew it was over.

"No," said Benjamin T. Stanton Jr. "I don't believe you."

And Lori gazed around the paintings on the walls and the deceased Stantons didn't believe her, either. "Then there's nothing more to say, is there?"

"So come on. The cake. Everybody's waiting." As if their previous exchange had not occurred.

"I can't." Lori slipped her hands out of Ben's. "If you don't believe me, you don't trust me, and if you don't trust me . . ."

"Forget all that," Ben dismissed urgently. "We can talk more later if you want to, but right now we're needed outside. Let's go. Lori . . ."

Shaking her head sorrowfully. "I'm sorry, Ben. No." Backing away, leaving him alone and puzzled and surrounded by his ancestors. "You're on your own."

"Fine. Great. So much for loyalty. What about you trusting me, Lori? What about that? All right, I'll do it myself. I don't need you. I can do it myself. Lori?" A final, faint appeal. "Fine."

He turned on his heel and went. Lori didn't seem able to

move. She felt too weary to move, so she stayed where she was. And from where she was, she could hear applause and cheers as if something of importance was taking place beyond her vision, and then there were voices raised in "Happy Birthday" and then "For He's a Jolly Good Fellow," but it all seemed so far off and distant that she couldn't believe that any of it truly mattered, or that it had anything to do with her.

Anything at all.

CHAPTER THREE

Cally had never been so pleased to see the walls of Deveraux Academy in her entire life. Actually, "pleased" was too small a word to describe her emotion as the school came into view. Ecstatic, maybe. Or enraptured. Something on a par with hallelujah.

The return journey from Newport to Spy High had not been pleasant, not with Ben staring stonily at Lori the whole way and Lori apparently fascinated by the floor. It might have been more comfortable had the stretch hoverlimo been able to stretch itself a little longer, to keep the silent members of Bond Team farther apart, but the atmosphere between them was so cold that Cally half-expected to develop a case of frostbite simply from sharing the same space. They'd known that something was wrong between Ben and Lori when she hadn't shown up for the cake-cutting last night, but nobody had yet dared to ask for details. Jake looked like he might have an idea, but he was being as tight-lipped as anyone. Indeed, all three of them were out of the limo and into the school almost before the vehicle had stopped.

"See you later, then, guys, you've been great company. Bye." Eddie watched them rush off reflectively. "Hey, Bex, Cal, you don't think I should change my deodorant, do you?"

"What deodorant?" sniffed Bex.

"I'm just glad we're back," sighed Cally, stretching extravagantly as she paced the gravel driveway outside Deveraux's main entrance. "All I want now is a few nice easy days in the classroom. No trauma. No crises."

"Don't hold your breath, Cal," grinned Bex, indicating

Violet Crabtree tottering out toward them and calling her name as if a national emergency had just been declared.

"Uh-oh," moaned Cally. Big, meaningless smile: "Hello, Mrs. Crabtree. Do you want me?"

The elderly receptionist chuckled like she knew a secret. "Somebody does. Somebody's here to see you."

"Really?" Cally was intrigued despite herself. "Who?"

"I told him you might not be back until later but he said he'd wait."

"Who, Mrs. Crabtree?"

"He's doing some work in the IGC research suite. That's where he'll be."

Old Violet must have made a great secret agent in her day, Cally thought. There was no getting anything out of her that she didn't want to reveal. Try again, anyway: "Who?"

"Mac Luther, of course," said Violet Crabtree, as if Cally should have known.

"Mac? Mac's here?" Delight lit up Cally's whole face. Suddenly, the painful limo journey seemed like old news. "Thanks, Mrs. C.!" And she ran into the school.

Eddie stared after her in puzzlement, then down at the six suitcases the chauffeur had just finished unloading from the trunk. "Okay, was this all a cunning plan to leave us with the luggage?"

"Who's Mac Luther?" Bex asked interestedly. "Boyfriend?"

"Not quite," said Eddie. "Mac's a Spy High Selector Agent. Picked Cally out while she was still on the streets. She stayed at a refuge place he runs. Learned a lot of her computing skills there."

"I thought Grant found her in a prison cell," Bex said.

"That's right. Cal was wild," Eddie acknowledged. "But who told Grant where to look? Nope, unless she's got a thing for older men that she's been keeping from us the last year and a half, I think Mac Luther's as close to a father figure as Cally's ever had."

"What a sensitive thing to say, Eddie." Bex patted his cheek. "Don't strain yourself with the bags now, will you?"

At first, Cally didn't notice what Mac Luther was watching on the viewing screens of the research suite. To begin with, he was all that mattered.

"Mac!" She threw her arms around him and hugged him close. "What are you doing here? It's so good to see you!"

"Yeah?" Mac laughed. "So why are you trying to suffocate me? Cally." He said her name with a parent's warmth. "Wasn't sure you'd still be here. They haven't sent you back to jail, then?"

"Oh, I'm a good girl now, didn't they tell you?" Cally smiled. "On the up and up. Weeks from graduation. I could break into the White House and steal the President's underwear if I wanted to."

"Not while he's still wearing it, I hope." Mac squeezed Cally's shoulder affectionately.

"They're saying I'm a credit to my Selector."

"You always were."

"Mac. I can't believe it." The battered boxer's face was still the same. Cally thought back to the times before Deveraux, before her present life in espionage, when she was struggling to survive on the streets of an oblivious city. She thought of the fate that seemed to have been marked out for her: crime, loneliness, and desolation. Then she thought of Mac and his faith in her, the first belief in her that anyone had ever shown, of the Refuge, her first real home. It had taken some getting used to and she'd learned only slowly, but she was a different Cally now, a better one. And she'd repay Mac's faith, every single day.

"Well, for a welcome like that, I ought to visit Deveraux more often," Mac was saying.

"Yeah, you should. So did you just come to see me, Mac, or —?"

"If only." For the first time, Mac's expression darkened, grew serious.

"Something wrong at the Refuge? If there's anything I can do to help . . ."

"Cally," said Mac, "what do you see on these screens?"

Green fields between arid rock, like an oasis in a desert. Circles of humble wooden buildings around a giant pyramid in stone and steel crowned by a cross. People in the fields, mainly young, late teens and twenties, working with their hands, working in simple robes, working with empty smiles and vacant eyes. Watched by older men and women garbed in white.

"The IGC's stock footage of Temple Prime," said Mac.

"Temple who?" Cally queried. "Is that a band or something?"

"Not quite. This is the earthly headquarters of the Temple of the Transformation."

"Mac, I don't want to sound like my brain's gone into terminal reverse since I left the Refuge, but I'm still not following. Temple of the Transformation? Who are they? A cult or something?"

"In one."

"Never heard of them."

"That's a pity, Cally, because what you were saying just then? If there's anything you could do to help? Well, there is."

Cally shrugged. "Name it."

Mac regarded her gravely. "I want you to join the Temple of the Transformation."

Ben knew what Senior Tutor Elmore Grant wanted. He'd been expecting such a summons for a while now. But the reality of it was still difficult to bear, and certainly nothing he felt like sharing with his teammates, not even Lori. *Especially* not Lori. He was deliberately shunning her for a while, avoiding her after her ridiculous accusations about Uncle Alex. She'd come back to him soon enough, and then he could do the gracious thing and forgive her.

So when the message came that Grant wanted to see him in his study and as a matter of some urgency, Ben slipped away stealthily, like Judas at the Last Supper.

Grant was all protocol and politeness. "Come in Ben. Take a seat. Make yourself comfortable. How was your party?"

"Excellent, thank you, sir." The niceties first, lulling him into a false sense of security. But if Ben kept the conversation on this level, perhaps he could avoid the inevitable. "And thank you again for allowing me a special leave of absence. And thank Mr. Deveraux, too, because —"

"I've been meaning to have this little chat with you for a while, Ben." No good. Grant was wise to that tactic. He was running his hands through his hair. Bad sign. "But I thought it was best to wait until after your birthday." Ben's file was open on the desk, like evidence.

"Sir?"

"It's your grades, Ben." The senior tutor sifted through accusing sheets of paper. "I'm afraid they're not as good as they were. I'm sure you must be aware of the fact."

"It's only a blip, sir, a temporary lapse. I might have taken my eye off the ball, but I can promise you that I'm going to be back to form as of now. I mean, back to my best." He dared to pause. Grant was silent. "You can trust me on that, sir."

Grant seemed to be reserving judgment. "This isn't simply about distractions, Ben, is it? Last year, your grades were exceptional, the highest average in the history of Deveraux Academy —" *So what's your problem?* Ben wanted to shout — "but this year there's been a steady decline in all areas of study, practical and theory."

He knew it. It was true. He thought of the cliff and the sky and how you could do anything if you were strong enough.

"Good students don't suddenly become bad students," Grant observed, "but good students can place themselves under so much pressure to achieve that in the end they crack under the strain. Is that what you feel is happening to you, Ben?" Casually but pointedly said.

"No, sir." He was swift in denial. "No way. I mean, not at all." Stantons didn't crack. Stantons stood tall while they had their portraits painted. "Like I said, it's just . . . temporary."

Grant ruminated. "Well, I don't need to remind you that your future career as a Deveraux operative is entirely dependent on success in your final examinations. No retakes. No second chances. Just like in the field." *Life or death*, thought Ben. *Graduate or mindwipe.* "And as it stands, your chances of passing are, I am afraid, in the balance. Unless you adopt strategies to arrest this —"

"I will, sir. You know I will." He was thinking of the Sherlock Shield, his pride in Bond Team's victory, their place in the Hall of Heroes. Was there a Lobby of Losers somewhere?

"Very well, Ben," said Grant calmly. "I'll be monitoring your performance over the next few weeks, and I'll expect to see an improvement. Because my one final suggestion is — and at this stage a suggestion is all it is — leadership of a team brings its own increased stresses and responsibilities. . . . If you wanted to step down as leader of Bond Team . . ."

"No, sir! Definitely not!" Ben could scarcely restrain himself from shouting.

"Very well, then," Grant acknowledged. "In that case, I think we're done. For now."

"Yes, sir. Thank you, sir." He couldn't wait to get out, to get away from the study, to be alone. He needed to think. He needed to remind himself who he was.

"And Ben," — Grant stopped him at the door, "don't think I've lost my faith in you. I haven't. Obstacles exist to be over- come. Bear that in mind. Overcome this one."

"Yes, sir," said Ben.

Not *join* them, join them, Mac had explained. Not actually *become* a disciple. Simply attend a meeting or service or whatever the Tem- ple called the ceremonies at their church near the Refuge. Pretend to be interested. Pose as a potential recruit. Then report back.

Cally had agreed, of course, because it was Mac asking her, but she didn't like it. She was suspicious of religions generally, of the answers they claimed to offer to human problems, of the way they had a habit of taking over and controlling people's lives. Cally believed that you had to make your own decisions, to place your trust in yourself and yourself alone. It vaguely amused her that she wasn't too far from Ben in that respect, re- gardless of their radically different backgrounds. So when she stood outside the church of the Temple of the Transformation, with the evening sky darkening and becoming the color of the surrounding disciples' robes, with the gathering, as it was apparently called, about to commence, and with an overnight pass from Deveraux in her jeans pocket, Cally was already an unlikely convert to the cause.

Her skepticism was reinforced by the kind of person herded into the church with her, to an encouraging chorus of "Step forward! Enter, dear friends! Transform your lives!" from the grinning disciples, like they were moonlighting from their day jobs organizing lines at theme parks. The congregation were young people, mostly. With lost faces and haunted eyes. Weak and willing to let somebody or something else take responsibility for them. There's nobody here to swell the ranks of Spy High, Cally thought grimly, as they shuffled to the pews. And Mac had been right. He'd have been too conspicuous to come to a gathering himself. Middle-aged men were not what the Temple was after. It was so much easier to exploit the young.

"Isn't this *wonderful!*" A girl at Cally's shoulder with colorless hair and pleading eyes, fingers that played nervously and constantly with her clothing, clearly wanted to strike up a conversation.

"Wonderful?" Cally fought to conceal her cynicism. "It's certainly something."

"Do you feel it, too?" The girl half-closed her eyes, the lids fluttering like wings. "Do you feel that sense of peace, like all our worries have been removed?"

"I think so," said Cally. Maybe the worries were going the same way as the girl's brains.

"It's hard, isn't it?" The girl appealed to Cally. "Finding

someone to trust. Everyone lets you down in the end, don't they? Parents, friends, boyfriends. You can't trust anyone."

"What about yourself?" Cally suggested.

The girl didn't seem to understand. "But Gabriel's different, isn't he? And the Temple. We can trust Gabriel and the Temple to look after us, and we won't need to worry anymore. You know, coming here —" the girl's fingers fiddled into overdrive "— feels like coming home."

Strange idea of home, thought Cally.

The interior of the church was broadly pyramidal, sharp and defined. There was no altar but a single giant screen set before the congregation. One of the disciples, a young man with pale, delicate features, like a doll, stood by the screen to address them. Cally noticed that the older disciples positioned themselves alongside the pews, scanning those seated in them as if preselecting the most suitable candidates for Temple membership. The young man's voice was as pale and delicate as the rest of him, like an invalid, but it had the strength to introduce an apparently endless supply of fellow disciples who all said much the same thing: that they'd been leading empty, aimless lives, that joining the Temple had changed them fundamentally, and that now they were fulfilled, reborn, *transformed*. It was like the largest commercial break in history.

Just as Cally began to feel rigor mortis setting in, Pale and Delicate drew to a close. Nearly. There was but one more speaker he needed to introduce, a speaker whose name he was unworthy to utter, a man who was no longer just a man — the blessed founder of the Temple of the Transformation, Gabriel himself. *Top of the bill time*, Cally thought. A cry of rapture rose from the assembled disciples. "Gabriel!" gasped the girl next to Cally, her face suffused with wonder. "Gabriel is going to speak to us!" Cally wondered whether the girl was carrying an autograph book.

But Gabriel's appearance was confined to the screen. A black man, early thirties, Cally estimated, good cheekbones, regal and austere, eyes that seemed tinged with gold, though you could do that easily enough with optical implants these days. He was robed in gold, too, like the sun. And he was impressive, Cally had to admit. There was presence and charisma, a voice that was seductively persuasive, a gaze that enthralled and entranced, a manner that seemed both powerful and compassionate. Cally held on to the fact that Gabriel's real name, as Mac had told her, was Calvin Johns. There could be nothing divine about a guy whose real name was Calvin Johns.

And essentially, Gabriel's message echoed that of his disciples: to find meaning in life, to gain true purpose and direction. The Temple could provide it all — through *Transformation*.

"Welcome, friend," said Pale and Delicate.

I'm not your friend, Cally thought. "Hi," she said. Mac had wanted her to find things out and now, as the gathering finally broke up and disciples and congregation mingled together, seemed as good a time as any.

"My name is Timothy," said Pale and Delicate, offering his hand.

"I'm pleased for you," said Cally, reluctantly taking it. It was like kneading yeast. "I'm Cally." She didn't relish revealing her name, but there seemed little choice.

"Cally." Said like he was filing it away for closer inspection later. "I was watching you from the front of the Temple, Cally, while our blessed founder was speaking. I saw the effect his words had on you, the inspiration they brought."

Yeah? Cally thought. *Best to get some laser treatment on those eyeballs then.*

"I've been lucky enough to meet Gabriel, you know, unworthy as I am."

"Is that right?" Cally admired, trying to keep the sarcasm to a minimum. "That must have been exciting for you."

"I could perhaps arrange it for you to meet the blessed founder, too, Cally," he hinted. "It is within my authority to send disciples from here to Temple Prime itself — to the very Temple of Tranquillity where Gabriel spends his days in contemplation and prayer. I have the power to do that."

"Really?" Cally gaped. "Wow."

"I share that with you, Cally, because I feel drawn to you," the disciple admitted. "I feel I can help you transform your life. I feel you have —" his eyes roamed over her from head to toe "— much to offer the Temple."

"You think so?" Cally was well into her gaping now. "Timothy, I don't know what to say."

A benign smile. "Perhaps we could go somewhere a little less crowded and talk some more. There are rooms in this Temple for study and reflection, private rooms . . ."

"Well, actually, I do know what to say," Cally corrected. "Not tonight, thank you. I've just remembered an appointment I've got with a friend. Nice meeting you though, Tim. Get well soon, you hear?" He'd confirmed all her suspicions. The Temple of the Transformation was just as bogus and manipulative as any other two-bit cult, and Timothy was a sleaze in black robes.

"But wait, Cally," he called after her. "Will we be seeing you again?"

"In your dreams," Cally muttered. And Mac had been worried about these guys? On the evidence of this evening, she couldn't understand why.

"Sister," a female disciple stepped in her path, "the time has come for Transformation."

Cally deftly avoided her, didn't even slow down. Transformation? Hardly. What the time had come for was a good hot shower.

Ben activated the touch-sensitive panel, and the lights came on in the main hall. At this time of night, it was empty, needless to say, but that was good. It was what Ben wanted. He wandered into the middle of the hall, such a familiar space to him now, and remembered his first sight of it, his first day at Spy High and the allocation of teams in this very place. Everybody had been a stranger then, everything new, and he remembered what he'd said to Jake: "Think like a winner or end up a loser." He'd been so certain that he'd succeed here. He couldn't falter in the final term. He couldn't allow it.

"Ben?" It was Lori. Of course. She must have been following him.

"Thought you wouldn't be able to stay away for long," he said. "Well, come on in and join me if you like. There's room. Something on your mind?"

"Oh, yes," said Lori. "Us."

"I'm listening." He faced her as she approached him in the center of the deserted hall. He'd been right. She was going to apologize now for her conduct at his party, admit she'd been wrong about Uncle Alex, beg his forgiveness. Ben felt his confidence returning.

"Do you know, this is where I first saw you," Lori said, looking around nostalgically.

"That's right. Grant's first little pep talk."

"We had to wear those stupid color-coded name badges, remember? And I don't know about you, but I was so nervous just being here and not really being certain what I'd let myself in for and not knowing anyone . . ."

"I wouldn't say I was exactly nervous," Ben qualified.

A wry smile teased Lori's lips. "But then I got talking to Cally and poor Jennifer, and then I saw Jake and Eddie. And then I saw you, Ben. The first time. You were standing . . ." Lori considered, let her memories return. "Actually, you were standing right where you are now, right there, only you had a glass in one hand and something on a stick in the other. And I thought you were the most gorgeous boy I'd ever seen."

"Can I have that in writing?" He'd already decided to forgive her. In his mind, they'd already made up. And he'd reclaimed his rightful position at the top of the team.

"And I was there just wondering what it'd be like to be your girl." Lori sighed. "It seems like a long time ago now. So much has happened since. Frankenstein. Nemesis, the Serpents, the Guardian Star. Jennifer. So much has changed."

"Not everything, though, Lori," Ben suggested. "Not us."

"Haven't we?"

Lori gazed at him with unflinching honesty, and for the first time Ben felt uneasy, unclear. "What do you mean, Lo?"

"I mean . . . I think we got together too soon, before we

really knew each other. I mean that I think we expected too much from each other. I mean it isn't working out."

"Isn't . . . ? You and me? That's stupid, Lori."

She shook her head. "You know it's not. You know it's true. Ben, when was the last time you confided in me, trusted me with a secret? Let me in? You don't seem to want me to be a full part of your life, and if you don't want that, I'm sorry, but you can't really want me at all."

"Lori, listen." There was an edge of panic in his voice. "If this is about my birthday . . ."

"That was part of it," said Lori, "but I've felt excluded for a long time now. I just haven't faced up to it. It's always been Ben and Lori —"

"It still can be."

"It can't." Lori was sad but sure. "It can't, Ben. As of now, there is no Ben and Lori. I'm sorry."

"I'll change then, if that's what you want. I can change."

"Ben, you're you."

"It's Jake, isn't it?" Hurt curdled into a need to hurt. "You're ditching me for Daly, aren't you? Come on, Miss Let's Be Honest With Each Other? Be honest now."

"This has nothing to do with Jake," Lori denied, pained. "It's got nothing to do with anyone but you and me."

"You're a liar." Ben's bitterness accelerated. "I saw you with Daly at the party, remember? I bet you were planning this then, just waiting for an excuse. Go on. Tell me I'm right. I can take it."

"I'm leaving now, Ben. I'm not going to fight with you. Believe me, I *am* sorry. But our relationship *is* over. Get used to it."

"I won't need to. I won't need to get used to it because you'll be back." As Lori turned and hurried from the hall, not seeing the accusing finger Ben stabbed at her. "You'll be back because you can't do without me, Lori, you need me. You haven't got the strength to be on your own. I know you, you hear me?"

She didn't. Ben was alone. Nobody heard him. He had the hall all to himself.

Cally walked briskly toward the Refuge feeling good and looking forward to a nice long chat with Mac. It'd be just like old times. All she'd need to do first was reassure him that this new cult was exactly the same as all the others — a passing fad, nothing more. No one would trust the likes of Timothy ahead of Mac Luther. The Refuge had nothing to fear from the Temple of the Transformation.

Against the background of the night sky, she saw a sudden flickering light.

A building was on fire. A building nearby, she estimated, just a few blocks away. Sadly, not unusual in this part of town. Arsonists Anonymous used to hold their annual conference here. But a few blocks away in the direction in which she was heading.

Maybe it was her Spy High training kicking in — the successful secret agent's ability to anticipate likely outcomes — or maybe it was because her early life had taught her always to expect the worst, but Cally was breaking into a run and under her breath she was muttering, "Oh, no." She somehow sensed which building was burning.

The Refuge was in flames, the blaze blistering the darkness and gaining in intensity the entire time, as if growing in the confidence of destruction. Racing to it, Cally could hear glass shattering and the *whoosh* of furniture igniting from inside. She could see the Refuge's young residents, most of them in their pajamas, milling around helplessly in the street, some clasping each other, others crying out or sobbing. Several had their arms up to protect them from the heat.

Nowhere could she see Mac Luther.

"What happened? What happened?" She seized on two girls who looked like sisters, shuddering and blinking as if experience as a whole was too much for them.

"We don't know. We were in bed. Stacey smelled burning. The Refuge. The Refuge was burning." Trauma had reduced the girl to the obvious.

The fire roared, like a beast devouring its prey.

"What about Mac?" Cally persisted. "Where's Mac?" The girl didn't seem to understand the question. Cally shook her. *"Where is Mac?"*

"Inside," the girl whimpered. "He's still inside."

The flames were scorching but Cally was cold, as cold as death. Still inside? "Mac!" she screamed. "Mac!"

But if he hadn't got out by now then he was either already . . . no. Not an option there. He could still be saved. He *would* be saved. Someone just had to go in there and pull him out.

"Hold on, Mac," Cally urged. "I'm coming."

CHAPTER FOUR

They saw where she was heading, and some of them might have guessed why. Cally heard them clamoring, shouts of warning, yells of alarm. One boy even tried to physically restrain her. "It's no good!" he kept repeating. "It's no good!" But she pushed him aside and, as she neared the flames, he didn't follow.

Deep breaths. Deep breaths. Relax internally. Fill those lungs with sweet, cool air. Cally tuned in to her training. Spy High graduates might have to function in any number of hostile environments, from ocean deeps to outer space. They'd learned to do without oxygen for as long as humanly possible, preferably longer. A few puffs of smoke would not be a problem.

And clear the mind. Don't ask yourself how the fire started. No questions. Successful missions were about answers. Remember the exact layout of the Refuge. Remember it so perfectly that if you were blind you could still find your way to Mac's office and out again. Because at this time of night, that was where Mac would be. In his office. Maybe he was just finishing off some paperwork now. Cally wished.

The fire was searing her skin already. She had to block out the pain, reject it. Pain was only physical. It could be mastered by the mind. The flames would not beat her back. She was an agent of Spy High, and she could not be stopped.

To an outburst of wails and screams from behind her, Cally plunged into the Refuge.

The main hallway first, past reception, through a tunnel of fire. Her clothes smoldered but she had to go forward, there was no going back. She kept to the middle of the passage, as far from the flames as possible. Their movement was dictated by science, by predictable currents of air. Cally could always improvise, do the unexpected. Her ability to think was what would keep her alive.

She turned left toward the administrative areas.

There was a fire door off its hinges. *Don't ask why*, she commanded herself. *Store the fact for debriefing later.*

All the doors were wide open, welcoming the fire inside. And the smoke was thicker here. Cally kept low. Smoke inevitably rose. She defended her lungs against it.

Fourth on the right was Mac's office. The open door at least meant she didn't have to worry about a backdraft.

But she did have to worry about the body sprawled on the carpet.

No sound, she instructed. *Don't call his name even though you want to. Emotional outbursts wouldn't help Mac, and they wouldn't preserve the precious air supply. Think practically. And simply register the overturned chairs, the scattered books, and broken desk lamp. If there'd been a fight here, it wasn't relevant now.*

Cally knelt by Mac's side, turned him over. His head was slick with blood and swollen with recent bruises, contusions. He hadn't just fallen while attempting to flee the fire. She felt for a pulse, trying to do so clinically, without panic. Found it. Faint, like a signal from someone lost and distant, but secure. Mac was alive.

It was down to her to keep him that way.

She grabbed his arms, hauled his limp body into a kind of sitting position, then clasped him around the back and strove to lift him from the floor. Her muscles almost tore in protest but she was strong, her training had made her strong, and despite the strain she would not give up. She twisted around so that her back was next to Mac. She leaned forward and took his weight on her, his dangling arms across her chest. Blinded by smoke and sweat, her limbs feeling like they were on fire themselves, Cally dragged the unconscious form of Mac forward, out of his office, toward the outside, toward safety.

But the heat was increasing now, and even bent nearly double as she was, Cally could find no clean air. She began to cough. She felt her lungs shriveling like overcooked meat. And there was new danger with each agonizing step into the hallway — the Refuge had not been constructed with the finest materials, and now its ceilings recognized defeat, cracked and crumbled. Chunks of burning masonry crashed to the floor, obstacles in Cally's path. She looked up once. Just as well. She staggered to the side to avoid debris that would have rendered her as senseless as Mac.

But the effort of her sudden lurch unbalanced the burden on her back. Cally felt Mac's body slipping. She tried to compensate, went down on one knee. A sharp pain jolted through her. And now she had to rise again, to stand once more, to keep going, and Mac was a weight that she could tolerate no longer. Yet she had to. She had to stand. Mac's life depended on her.

She *would* stand. She would walk. Mac had selected her for Spy High, and tonight she'd show him he'd been right.

Cally braced herself, mustered all her might, her purpose, her will. She cried out. She screamed out. She pushed herself up.

And she stood. And though Mac was still heavy, Cally knew that the crisis was past. She could carry him the final few meters to the door. She stumbled on, undaunted. The inferno would not claim them. They would leave. They would live.

And then Cally would be looking for a very cold drink.

IGC Data Search X40

Key: The Temple of the Transformation

Requested: Selector Agent Macready Luther

Footage: ILC TV interview with parents of Alice Hodge.

"She was such a good girl. The perfect daughter. You couldn't have hoped for a better daughter.

"Alice had plans. University. A career. She wanted to be a doctor. She wanted to help people. I don't understand . . .

"She was happy. She was full of life. And she was a normal girl, until she met – what do they call themselves? *Disciples?* They're not fit to say the word. *They're evil.* Predators. They took my baby from us. . . .

"As soon as Alice got involved with this Temple of the Transformation, she changed. It was like a light going out. It was like they'd brainwashed her or something. And now she's gone to join some mindless commune or whatever, and the authorities tell us there's nothing we can do. They tell us we can't even act to save our own daughter. I don't understand. The world's gone mad. It's all gone mad."

Footage: H-NET interview with "Gabriel."

"We force no one to join us. No one. Ask any of our disciples, and they will tell you the same: They came to the Temple of the Transformation out of their own free will. They joined us to be changed, to be transformed as I was when the herald of the Lord spoke to me and brought me to this place and bade me to build a new religion to redeem the world. For the people of the world have lost their way, and their only hope lies in Transformation, to turn their backs on their past, to turn their backs on their families, to be born again with a new name and a new destiny as disciples of the Temple. Our numbers are rising every day, praise the Lord, and they will continue to rise. The time of Transformation is upon us, and to those who resist, to those who stand in our way –" the golden eyes glittered "– a reckoning will come."

"So," Jake edged cautiously, "there's no change in Mac's condition yet?"

Cally swirled her coffee around in its cup, made no attempt to sip it. "No. He still hasn't regained consciousness."

"That doesn't mean to say he won't, though," Bex encouraged. "I mean, people come out of comas all the time these days, don't they? I hear there's even hope for Eddie."

"Charming," grunted Eddie. "But Bex is right, Cal. And at least we know with Mac here, he's going to get the best possible treatment available. He'll get through this, don't you think, Ben?" Inviting the final member of Bond Team present in the recreation room to express his agreement with the optimism of his teammates.

Ben nearly didn't. With his own problems on his mind he nearly said: "What do I look like to you, a doctor?" But not even Ben on a bad day was as insensitive as that. Instead he managed, "Sure. Don't worry, Cal. Mac'll be fine."

"Well, the person who did that to him won't be when I catch up with them," Cally vowed darkly. "I know it was no accident. You didn't need to be from Spy High to see that. Mac was beaten. The fire at the Refuge was started deliberately."

"But by who?" Jake asked. "And why?"

"My money's on the Temple." If Cally squeezed her coffee cup any more tightly, it was going to crack. "I told you he was worried about them, how they were moving in."

"You also told us that you didn't find anything particularly suspicious at this gathering you went to," reminded Ben.

"Maybe I didn't look closely enough. Maybe I was fooled."

"Well, Mac'll be able to tell us more himself when he recovers," Jake said.

"Enough with the looking-on-the-bright-side agenda," Cally retorted. "I know you mean well and thanks, but that's *if* Mac recovers. And I don't plan on waiting until whenever that might be. I plan on taking a second trip to the Temple as soon as I can get a pass, and this time I won't be smiling."

"Hold on, Cal," warned Ben. "What about evidence? You can't just go sneaking around private property without good reason."

"Is that right?" scorned Cally. "And you think I care?"

"Listen." Ben found himself leaning forward, committing himself to the argument as if he did care. "They've got the traces of skin they found under Mac's fingernails, right? Not his own, therefore likely to be his assailant's — probably clawed off during the fight. And now they're trying to do a DNA match with our database of known criminals. Cally, at least wait until you know the results of that. I mean, the Temple could have nothing to do with this. Your friend's Refuge isn't exactly in the best of neighborhoods, is it? There must be criminal activity all the time —"

"That's right, Ben, all the time," Cally mocked, "but at least where you live, you don't have to look at any of it, do you?"

"Hey, I didn't mean —"

"Where's Lori?" Bex thought it was wise to change the subject. "Ben?"

"How should I know?" The defensiveness of his tone alerted his teammates. "I'm not Lori's keeper, am I?" *I'm not even her boyfriend anymore, he thought bitterly.* It was the moment he'd been dreading all day, the inevitable moment. Telling the others that he and Lori had split, broken up, gone their separate ways, were an item no longer. It had to be done, and their eyes were on him. "Actually, there's something I guess you ought to know . . ."

"Hi, guys." And then their eyes weren't on Ben but raised and gazing behind him. "I'm back." It was Lori. So why was everyone staring as if they'd never seen her before? Ben turned. Stared, too.

A new Lori stood before them. Her signature long hair, her beautiful tide of long, blonde hair, was gone. She was shorn. Her hair was short now, fringing her forehead and curling just below her ears.

Lori laughed at her friends' surprise. "Did you miss me?"

"I can't believe it." Bex seemed unable to stop shaking her head, even though that made her simultaneous application of mascara, purple to match her hair, a treacherous business. "Ben and Lori. Lori and Ben. You know, your names have always gone together ever since I've been at Spy High. Like Romeo and Juliet, or Bonnie and Clyde . . ."

"Thank *you*," said Lori from her recumbent position on her bed. "And we all know what happened to *them*."

"No, what I meant was," Bex blinked approvingly at herself in the mirror, "what I meant was, I just can't believe the two of you have split up."

"You haven't known Ben as long as the rest of us, Bex," commented Cally acidly from the chair by the door. "I can't believe you stayed together as long as you did, Lo."

The girls were in their room. It was Friday night and the regular holoclub was only minutes away.

"That's not fair, Cal," rebuked Lori.

"Absolutely." Bex finalized her jewelry. "All right, so Ben can be full of himself sometimes — he's a boy, right? Boys have to have big egos to make up for deficiencies elsewhere. But he sure looks good in a shock suit, doesn't he? Nice buns."

"Ben's buns," Lori couldn't help grinning, "are back on the market."

"So you want to tell us why the big bye-bye, Lo? Grisly details compulsory."

"No, I don't, thank you, Bex." The grin turned out to be temporary. A frown slunk across Lori's features to replace it.

"But the new look — I bet your neck's feeling the cold after all this time, isn't it? — that's something to do with it, right? Fresh start?"

"Let me just find a couch to lie on and you can continue your analysis, Dr. Deveraux."

"Well, at least tonight ought to cheer you up. And who knows? Ben's not the only one back on the market."

"Actually," Lori sat up, "I'm not sure I feel up to dancing tonight. I think I might stay here. . . ."

"Don't say and wash your hair," Bex snorted. "That old chestnut won't do. It'll only take you five minutes now, anyway."

"I'm not coming, either," declared Cally. "I'm going to sit with Mac a bit. I need some time to think." She'd already decided — grudgingly — that Ben was right about delaying action until the DNA tests were concluded. Seemed even the son of the Stantons could talk sense once in a while.

"Well, that settles it, then. I can't go on my own," Bex moaned. "Lori, you've *got* to come. Don't leave me alone with Eddie. Please!"

Lori raised her hands in surrender. "All right, Bex, you win. Just don't expect me to enjoy it *or* start looking for someone else.

From now on, Lori Angel's on her own." She hoped it sounded convincing.

Ben used to be first at the holoclub, keen to be in the center of the dance floor with Lori very visible on his arm. But he figured those days were probably gone, and he certainly wouldn't show his face tonight. The grapevine at any school was good, but at a school for secret agents, it was positively psychic. Everyone would know that Stanton and Angel had split up. Everyone would be watching him, whispering; some might even be smirking. Ben did not feel like enduring the inevitable taunts of Simon Macey, for one. And he didn't think he could bear the sight of Lori if she went, either, dancing out of reach, laughing with others with her back to him. No, it was best to stay away. He had more pressing priorities right now, in any case.

The examination center was hardly the most popular room in the school at the best of times, and was shunned as a leper on Friday nights, but Ben didn't care. He settled himself into one of the leather chairs, like airline seats but with more controls in the arm rests, and activated the cyberhelmet above. It descended smoothly to cover his skull, clicked into place beneath his chin, the visor across his eyes. If his marks were low, he needed to raise them up again. That meant practice tests. Ben keyed in "Ciphers and Codes." The cyberhelmet linked the wearer's mind directly to the examinations computer, which tested and graded the students. It was quick and it was efficient, but the candidate had to be absolutely and entirely focused. Just as on a mission, there was no room for error.

And Ben used to be an expert at this, his mind sharp and his purpose clear. Nothing else used to matter to him but the test. But now, as the computer fed code after code into his brain, he felt that clarity slipping, muddied by other considerations. He ought to be registering only the lists of letters, symbols, and numerals that he needed to shape into meaningful language. He ought not to be seeing Lori's face, not now. It was distracting him. It was disturbing him.

A line inched like a scarlet worm across his vision. That was a problem. If he red-lined completely, that meant he'd failed the test. And failure was not an option.

Ben renewed his application. Focus. Concentrate. He could do it. Despite Lori, he would not be beaten.

But all the while, the red line lengthened. . . .

Club Night was really starting to heat up as band after band took to the floor to do its thing. At least, as holograms of the bands made an appearance.

Eddie Nelligan's mind, however, was on somebody very much of flesh and blood. "There's Bex over there," he pointed out, nudging Jake so vigorously that he almost spilled his drink. "Doesn't she look great?"

Jake nodded, trying not to notice Lori with her, looking nervous, looking gorgeous.

"I think tonight's the night," Eddie was confiding with relish. "I think I've kept her dangling long enough. It's time to make a move." Jake wished him luck. And meant it. "You could be in there as well. Now that Ben's off the scene. Lovely girl like Lori won't want to dance alone."

"Shut up, Eddie," Jake snapped automatically, even though

he was right. No Ben. No obstacle. And was Lori glancing across toward him? Was she averting her gaze shyly as he looked back?

"They're eyeing us," Bex was observing from the other side of the room. "Does Eddie *ever* get the message? Oh, well, I suppose determination against all the odds is a useful quality in a secret agent. Still won't get him where he wants to go, though. But Jake's looking lean and mean, wouldn't you say, Lori?"

"Don't know. You obviously would." Lori seemed not to care.

"Yeah, and I'm not the one who can hardly take my eyes off him," Bex grinned. "Go on, girlfriend. What are you waiting for?"

"You're full of you know what, Bex," declared Lori.

"Yeah? So you won't mind if I turn the Deveraux charm on to our resident tall, dark, and handsome?" Lori's eyes sparked blue fire. "Oh," Bex chuckled, "so I take it you *do* mind but don't want to admit it."

"Take it any way you want, Rebecca," Lori snapped uncomfortably. "I'm going to get a drink."

Anything to be alone. The music was loud. She couldn't think. Lori shoved through the holographic singer on the way to the bar. He didn't seem to mind. She knew she should have stayed in her room. And in her room she maybe wouldn't have had to feel guilty. Guilty because although she knew she'd been right to break up with Ben, she knew deep down that he'd been partly right as well.

She could sense Jake's eyes on her. The other students flitted between them, laughing, cheering, having to shout to make themselves heard above the pulse of the music. They were like extras in a movie. They were background. Only she and Jake were important.

Was he smiling at her? Was she smiling at him? Were they moving closer now, magnetized, mesmerized?

She felt a hand on her shoulder.

"Lori." But it was the oily, sneering features of Simon Macey that she was forced to face. "I understand commiserations are in order, or should that be congratulations? You've finally given Stanton the bullet, I hear. I guess after all this time you finally realized you couldn't compete with his own reflection, right?"

"What do you want, Simon?" Lori asked coldly. She remembered last year and what Macey had put her through during the competition for the Sherlock Shield. It was not a happy memory.

"Only to offer my services. In the spirit of Solo Team–Bond Team cooperation." How had she even been taken in by that woefully false smile? "You know, to help you get over Ben. I'm always available."

"Get lost, Simon." She didn't even try to be witty, just dismissed him and turned her attention back toward . . .

Jake had gone. Lori felt a strange sense of panic, a pang of loss. Where was he? She scoured the disco, but secret agent eyes missed nothing. Jake wasn't there. It was just as well that Simon Macey had moved off, or he might have regretted his brief intervention. Lori sighed, and she was surprised at how deeply. There was no longer any point in her remaining here. She wasn't a big fan of twentieth-century music anyhow, and without Jake . . . Across the floor, she saw Bex and Eddie fooling around like they were having a good time. Clubs could be lonely places if you weren't. Nobody would notice her slipping out.

It was cooler in the corridor. The music fell away. The perspiration on Lori' skin dried and made her shiver.

And then fingers brushed her arm.

"Simon, I thought I told you —," Lori whirled angrily.

But this time it wasn't Simon Macey. This time it was Jake.

Red-lined. Totally.

Ben slumped in the chair in a mixture of shock and dismay. He was losing it. He had to be honest with himself and face up to the truth. He was losing it big-time. Even worse, he didn't know what to do about it.

But of course, if he was honest with himself, he would know exactly what to do.

Go to Lori. Trust her. Confide in her. As he should have done from the start. Tell her everything. Tell her about the pressure, the relentless pressure to be the best. How it was constantly driving him on, obsessing him, consuming his life.

He had to do it now. There was no choice. He'd go to Lori, he'd talk to her, *he'd* apologize to *her*, and he'd tell her everything. And she'd understand. Lori always understood. And she'd hold him, and there'd be kissing and stuff, and she'd take him back, and they'd be together again as they were meant to be.

And everything would be all right.

"No, honestly, Eddie, it's fine. Thank you. I've been able to open doors since I was sixteen months old. I don't think the one to my room is gonna break my sequence."

"No. No. I insist. All part of the service. You got a key, though? Hey, it opens anyway. Don't need the key."

"It's pitch black, though." Bex frowned, reached for the light switch.

"Maybe you forgot to lock it."

"I never forget," Bex said, "anything . . ."

Cally was sitting on her bed, as still as a corpse. Her hands rested on her knees. Her expression bleak, like a distant moor.

"Hey, Cal," Eddie said curiously, "you all right?"

Bex was quicker. "Is it Mac?"

Cally adjusted her gaze to include her teammates, though it was as if she scarcely saw them. "He's dead," she said colorlessly. "Mac died an hour ago."

CHAPTER FIVE

Cally hadn't slept all that night. Hadn't bothered to try. She'd spent the hours since midnight on a lonely vigil in the Spy High Data Analysis Center, waiting for the skin extracted from underneath Mac's fingernails to find a DNA match. Waiting to learn the identity of his attacker.

The tech administering the program hadn't slept, either, and he didn't have Cally's burning rage to help him keep awake. His head was beginning to droop. His spectacles were slipping down the bridge of his nose.

Every ten minutes or so, he repeated the same words: "You don't have to stay, you know. This could take hours yet."

And Cally's reply was always the same: "I'll wait."

The tech had eventually succumbed to slumber. He lolled in his chair at a physically unsustainable angle and muttered in his sleep. He'd ache when he woke.

So he wasn't conscious when the screen flashed white with success, when the three vital words DNA MATCH SECURED appeared in accusing crimson, like blood, or when the picture and personal details of one Jarrett Jensen were downloaded from the database.

Cally, on the other hand, was aware of it all. Very aware.

The tech woke up alone, shifting uncomfortably in his chair. Maybe Cally had finally taken his advice and gone to bed in her own room. Or maybe she hadn't.

Jarrett Jensen's details had included his current address.

* * *

A good secret agent should never take things personally, Cally remembered as she SkyBiked toward the city and Jensen's apartment. The bike's navigation systems had already located it. A good secret agent should always remain emotionally detached from his or her mission in order to facilitate cool, calm decision making. But Cally also remembered Mac Luther, his rich, mellow laugh, the love in him for life's losers, the wise smile on his battered face. And another face was etched in her brain now: the sharp, sneering face of Jarrett Jensen. A thug with convictions for burglary, assault, and armed robbery. And she wasn't really on a mission, anyway, not *officially*.

A good secret agent should never take things personally. Unless, of course, they *were* personal.

Jensen's apartment building was gray and anonymous. It was still early morning. With any luck, she'd find him inside, maybe still asleep. He was in for a rude awakening.

Cally parked the SkyBike, demobilized it. As she mounted the stairs to Jensen's floor, she realized that she'd left Spy High without equipping herself with any weapons. She doubted it would matter, though a small voice in the back of her mind reminded her that a good secret agent should always be fully prepared when embarking on operations. Cally figured she wouldn't need artificial aids to deal with a second-rate scumbag like Jensen.

Just as she didn't need electronic assistance to pick the lock to his apartment. Locked from the outside, unfortunately, so Jensen wasn't home. Oh, well, an unexpected visitor would be a nice surprise for him.

Cally entered the apartment, checked it out. Empty, and in such disarray that if it wasn't so unlikely she might have suspected the place had recently been ransacked. Pacing the rooms impatiently, it was all she could do to stop herself from contributing further to the chaos, from maybe smashing Jensen's videoscreen, the unwashed crockery in his kitchen, from splintering his cheap furniture with her bare hands. The frustration in her was craving release . . .

"Who the hell are you?"

A good secret agent should be as much aware of what is happening behind her as of what might be unfolding before her.

Cally wheeled. A man with a sharp, sneering face stood in the doorway. Jarrett Jensen had come home.

"Me?" Cally's muscles bunched. "I'm a friend of Mac Luther's."

Jensen's hand was inside his jacket. Shoulder holster. Shock blaster.

Cally sprung him before he could let off a shot, ramming into him, slamming him into the wall. Plaster flaked like dandruff. A karate blow paralyzed his right arm, forcing him to drop the blaster. Then Cally threw him, sent him sprawling on the floor. And then she was kneeling across his chest, pinning him down, feeling his ragged breathing, the rise and fall of his chest.

"Okay, okay!" If Jensen could have raised his arms, he probably would have done so. "I give in! I give up!"

Cally was disappointed. She'd have preferred to hit him some more. Even though a good secret agent should never expend energy unnecessarily.

"Where did a kid like you learn those moves?" Jensen gaped. "Who the hell are you?"

"I'm the one asking the questions," Cally glared, "and there's one in particular: When you left Mac Luther for dead and torched the Refuge, was that your own idea or did somebody else put you up to it?"

"I have no idea what you're talking about," Jensen denied.

"Not an answer that's making me happy." Cally pressed down harder on the man's chest. "Tell me something worth hearing or I won't need you around anymore."

"Okay, okay. Just . . . okay."

Jensen was gasping. Thinking she might have gone too far, Cally relaxed. Slightly. Briefly.

It was Jensen's turn to throw her. With a sudden heave, surprisingly strong, he pushed her off him, a wild swing of his fist catching her cheek, stunning her momentarily. He was scrambling to his feet, lunging for the shock blaster, for the door. Cally rolled and was up, but he'd reached them both before she could prevent it. The blaster fired. Cally dived. The videoscreen exploded. And Jensen was gone.

But not far. Anticipating what was coming, Cally threw herself through the doorway and into the corridor, keeping low so that the shock blast, its trajectory assuming her normal height, crackled harmlessly above her. Jensen did not wait around for another try. She saw him launching himself down the stairs.

After him. Get up and after him.

Cally was gaining as she took the stairs in great leaps, but there weren't sufficient flights between the two of them and the ground for her to make her pursuit skills count. Jensen would exit the building before her.

But not by much. He was in a Wheelless, already powering up its magnetic engine, pulling out into the road. He waved to her and jeered from the vehicle's open window. Obviously he knew the acceleration on the Wheelless would soon put him way beyond her reach.

Cally vaulted onto her SkyBike. *We'll see about that,* she

thought. The bike reared into life. She gripped the handlebars as tightly as she wished she'd squeezed Jensen's neck. He was already a blur in the distance.

But not for long. She could not, would not allow Mac's murderer to escape. Whatever it took.

Everybody seemed to be missing this morning. Eddie might have been enjoying one of the celebrated Nelligan Saturday sleep-ins, but Jake was nowhere to be seen (not that Ben could bring himself to feel very unhappy about that). And when he dropped by the girls' room, its sole occupant turned out to be Bex. She told him about Mac's death and Cally going to the Data Analysis Center. Ben's sympathies were real — he imagined that losing Mac was to Cally what losing Uncle Alex would be to him — but his immediate priority remained Lori. Before the strength to apologize failed him. Unfortunately, Lori had vanished before Bex had even stirred this morning, she didn't know where to. Ben thanked her anyway. "Politeness, Ben?" Bex marveled. "Not sickening for something, are you?"

He made deductions and headed outside, into the school's grounds. Lori had to be regretting their breakup, had to be. She couldn't just turn her back on all they'd meant to each other and carry on with her life regardless. She'd be thinking about him, about them, and she'd be doing it somewhere that had been special to the two of them.

Like the gazebo. The gazebo where they'd sat and talked and put their arms around each other. And Ben was right, of course. Even from a distance, he could make out Lori, who was continuing to do exactly what they'd used to do together, only now with somebody else. It numbed Ben in his tracks. Somebody else's arm. Somebody else held close. He wished his eyesight was not so good.

Jake and Lori seemed very friendly.

He couldn't believe it. It was what he'd always secretly dreaded, and somehow it had come true. Lori and *Jake*. Daly had made his move. He'd taken advantage of Lori's vulnerability. He was using her in her moment of weakness.

But what could Ben do about it? Charge up to them now in indignant anger, tear them apart, challenge Jake to a duel? Reckless and stupid, neither attributes to be encouraged in a Spy High team leader. Ben was already shrinking back the way he'd come. They hadn't seen him. He could afford to bide his time. But sooner or later, he and Jake Daly would have words.

"You can't mean it," Ben didn't hear Jake saying. "Why not? You ashamed of me or something?"

"Don't be ridiculous," Lori scolded laughingly. "I want everyone to know we're together, of course I do, but just not right now. I hurt Ben badly enough splitting up with him. If we go public immediately, it'll be like rubbing salt in the wound."

"I can live with that," Jake teased.

"No, you can't."

"He'll have to find out sometime." More serious now. "He's just going to have to get used to the fact."

"I know," said Lori, "but I want to tell him in my own way, in my own time. Ben deserves that much. Let's keep it quiet for just a little longer."

The Wheelless was fast, and Jarrett Jensen clearly knew how to handle it, but all the while they were restricted to city roads, the advantage lay with the sleeker, more maneuverable SkyBike. Cally intended to make that count.

Her concentration was absolute. She hunched forward in the saddle, the wind streaming her dreadlocks out behind her, her total mastery of the bike permitting her to flit through traffic as if it was a geriatric. The outraged horns and shaking fists of other drivers she ignored, scarcely saw. If she'd had time, she might have grinned. Even with the Wheelless's Object Avoidance Systems evidently fully functional, even with running red lights and streaking across junctions, the routine congestion of the city was slowing Jensen down. She was catching him. And soon, she'd have him.

Jensen must have reached the same conclusion. Otherwise, why would he suddenly change his tactics, sacrificing a little speed to engage the automatic driver and thrusting his head and half his upper body out of the vehicle's window to shoot at his pursuer with his shock blaster? Sign of desperation, Cally thought with grim satisfaction. Because the blasts would never hit her. In the old days, when she'd have only had the option of veering her bike to the right or to the left, she might have been in trouble. But now she could dart up or down as well, making herself a very difficult target.

Then she realized with horror what Jensen was really doing. He wasn't aiming at her at all. He was shooting at the other cars, the innocent drivers. If he could cause a crash, it might block her path. An out-of-control vehicle might inadvertently collide with her and do his job for him.

A shock blast shattered a windscreen. The wounded Wheelless swerved, swung around so that its side was like a barrier in Cally's way. There were children inside. They were screaming. In seconds, she would be smashing into them, killing them.

No.

Cally pulled back on the handlebars, and the SkyBike surged higher, skimming the Wheelless's roof but passing harmlessly over it. There would be no fatalities as a result of Cally Cross's actions today. And Jensen had done enough damage already.

The bike shuddered beneath her as she forced its velocity to increase still further. The wind lashing against her now was almost blinding. But she was virtually alongside Jensen. He was grinning. The shock blaster gleamed. It couldn't miss from here.

But with one final burst of acceleration, the SkyBike spurted past the Wheelless. Jensen's shot scorched empty air. And then Cally was angling the bike across the larger vehicle. The Object Avoidance System saw it coming, reacted accordingly. Rather, as Cally had hoped, too quickly. The Wheelless spun, gravity and the laws of motion outwitting even the automatic driver, which was only a computer program in any case and didn't feel pain or a sense of failure. It left the road, couldn't avoid the nearest wall. The CARE function (Compressed Air Response to Emergencies) would protect Jarrett Jensen from the impact of collision. But it wouldn't protect him from Cally.

She dragged him dazed and shaken from the car, appropriated the shock blaster for herself this time, just to be on the safe side. Not that there appeared to be any fight left in Jensen now. Other vehicles were pulling up, their occupants getting out and observing the scene nervously, not quite daring to intervene. Cally needed information before the authorities arrived.

"So are we in a more talkative mood than we were before?" she demanded. "I for one sure hope so." She flourished the shock blaster. "Specialist subject: Mac Luther. You have thirty seconds starting now."

Jarrett Jensen groveled on the sidewalk. "I can't . . . I can't tell you. . . ."

"Sure you can," Cally encouraged darkly. "Twenty-five seconds."

"If I talk . . . they'll kill me."

"Who will?" Cally forced. "The Temple?"

"Temple? I don't know . . ." Jensen seemed genuinely puzzled. "What's the Temple? Listen, I had nothing against the guy. Is he a relative of yours or something?"

"Or something," said Cally. "And you've stopped talking."

"Okay, but it wasn't personal. It was just a job. But the people I work for, you don't want to cross them. You don't know how powerful they are."

"Who are they? Names."

"I'm telling you, you don't understand. These people, they run everything. They could have you and me disposed of just like that." He snapped his fingers for emphasis, almost like striking a flint. Very much like striking a flint. Almost imperceptibly, Jensen's clothes began to smolder. "If I betray them, I'm done for. You hear what I'm . . . saying . . . is that, say is that something burning . . . ? I . . ." Eyes bulging with realization. "Oh, my God, I told you! I'm done for!"

Cally stepped backward as Jensen scrambled to his feet. He was shuddering, though not from cold. Sweat dribbled down his forehead, and smoke was rising. *Not* from his clothes. From his *skin*.

"You've got to help me." He groped futilely toward Cally. "Please. Help me. It's the —"

But they were Jensen's final words. Instead of sound, a sudden, startling spout of flame erupted from his mouth, like a dragon's breath. His entire body went rigid. His entire body pitched forward, blackening and burning.

If Jarrett Jensen had been a steak, he'd have been extremely well done by the time he hit the sidewalk.

"Explosive implants," Senior Tutor Elmore Grant read from the medical report. "No doubt triggered to activate themselves if their host said certain words or phrases. I would imagine as soon as Jensen started to talk about his employers, he was signing his own death warrant."

"That's what I call going out with a bang," quipped Eddie.

"Horrible." Lori hugged herself as if it were suddenly cold.

Bond Team gathered with Grant and Corporal Keene in Briefing Room One to share intelligence and ideas concerning the deaths of both Mac Luther and Jarrett Jensen.

"Horrible indeed, Lori," agreed Grant, "and certainly proof that the attack on Mac was neither random nor a simple burglary that got out of hand. As a rule, burglars and petty criminals do not have explosive implants placed inside of them."

"Pity," grunted Ben. "That'd be one way of keeping crime down." He was all too aware of Jake sitting next to Lori. None of the others seemed to think this remarkable, but he knew what it meant. If there was a spare explosive implant going around, Ben had a use for it.

"But we still have no idea who might have been behind the attack," Grant was summarizing, "or, indeed, why."

"Do you think somebody could have known that Mac was a Deveraux Selector Agent?" Jake suggested.

"Of course not," Ben scoffed quickly. Too quickly, earning him some disapproving glances, the most hurtful from Lori. He'd been going to follow up with "That's a dumb idea," but decided against it.

"That's a possibility, Jake," accepted Grant, "but unlikely. Our cover is very good, and even if it were true, it's difficult to see what the purpose would be."

"I still think the Temple of Transformation is involved," Cally declared.

"Even though you said Jensen didn't seem to have heard of them and you believed him," Bex pointed out.

"And there's no suggestion in his records that he'd ever been linked with the Temple or with anyone known to be associated with it," Grant added.

"I know, I know." Cally shrugged. "I've just got a feeling, that's all."

"Oh, great." Ben found himself scoffing again, almost like he couldn't help it. "Forget the evidence. Let's just go on feminine intuition."

"On form today, Benny boy," noted Eddie.

"All right, all right," Corporal Keene intervened. "The briefing room is not the place for bickering."

"Absolutely, Corporal," said the senior tutor, fixing a warning gaze momentarily on Ben. "Now Cally may have a point. An agent's instincts are never to be wholly disregarded. But Ben has a point, too, when expressed more temperately. What do we know about Jarrett Jensen that could help us? Well, he was released from jail some three months ago and since then has been working at the Centennial Club in Boston."

"What?" Now Ben was too surprised to scoff. "That can't be right."

"Any reason why not?" Cally asked.

"You've got a feeling, right, Ben?" Jake couldn't resist.

"My parents are members of the Centennial Club," Ben said without a hint of irony. "I'm a member. Virtually the entire social elite of this country and others are members, anyone who's anyone. It's a very select institution. And it wouldn't be employing known criminals."

"Okay, then, we'd better start looking elsewhere, anywhere but at the rich guys," Jake said, very much *with* irony

"He said the people he worked for were powerful, that they ran everything," Cally recalled. "Jensen said that."

"So what? That could mean anything." Ben defended his class. "Some of the most respectable and philanthropic people alive are part of the Centennial Club. Are you accusing them of sending criminals out to burn down shelters for street kids for no apparent reason?"

"No *apparent* reason doesn't mean no reason at *all*, Ben," observed Lori, which was just what he needed.

"We're not as advanced as accusations yet, in any case," said Grant, "but it is undeniably true that Jensen worked at the Centennial Club, as a member of the cleaning staff, apparently."

"Maybe he polished the rich guys' thousand dollar shoes for them," said Jake.

"More interestingly," Grant pursued, "his employment records that the techs hacked in to claim that he was at work the night Mac was attacked, which we know cannot have been true."

"So either Jensen had the brains to fix his records and give himself an alibi," said Lori.

"Which I doubt." From Cally.

"Or somebody at the Centennial Club covered for him." Jake knew what he believed.

"Not necessarily," Ben protested. "We hacked into its system. Someone else could have, too."

"Agreed," said Grant, "but I think we have discovered an anomaly sufficient to justify a little infiltration and investigation of our own, if only to eliminate the Centennial Club from further inquiries. Ben, as an actual member of the club, perhaps you could —"

He was shaking his head already. "I'm not sure, sir. I don't think so."

"Ben?" Lori regarded him with concern. Ben Stanton *not* keen to volunteer for operational duty?

"I know too many people at the club. My parents. Relatives. Uncle Alex is chairman right now. I'd feel like I was spying on them."

"But, Ben," Cally pleaded, "what about Mac?"

He found the strength to look her in the eye. "I'm sorry, Cal. I just don't think I'm the right one to do it. You'll have to find someone else."

"There is no one else who's a member of the club," Grant pointed out gently.

"Well, actually, sir, that's not entirely true." Bex lifted her hand and waved it around a bit. "The Deverauxs have a kind of family membership, too. Course, Dad hasn't attended for a while, and I've never been, but there's a first time for everything. You want someone to snoop around the Centennial Club? Bex Deveraux is on the case."

CHAPTER SIX

IGC Data Library

File Name: The Centennial Club

Founded by railway magnate Leland Prescott on the hundredth anniversary of the Declaration of Independence, Boston's Centennial Club was originally intended to have an overtly political purpose, with membership tightly restricted to the one hundred most powerful and influential men in the land.

In the letter that Prescott sent to prospective members, he wrote that "a new age is upon us, an age of technology, an age of science, and those of us who are best equipped to shape that age must have a place to come together, a tranquil oasis removed from the daily business of our lives, a sanctuary where the great ideas of our times can be discussed and debated with those of like mind, to secure that the future path of our nation is built for the good of all." That place was to be the Centennial Club.

Over the years, and particularly with the death of Leland Prescott on the last day of 1899, the emphasis of the club began to change. Membership was extended beyond a hundred, women could join as well as men, and social and leisure activities slowly but surely replaced political debate as the central reason for attendance.

Nowadays, the Centennial Club no longer dominates East Coast society as it used to. Its movement from its original site to a new hightech building in downtown Boston in 2050 seemed only to reinforce its change of emphasis. In many ways, the Centennial Club is now no different from any other recreational meeting place, though it remains as exclusive as ever. Unless an applicant numbers among the wealthiest of the population, he will find the doors of the Centennial Club closed against him.

Bex felt out of place. Not just because the understated luxury of the Centennial Club's Prescott Lounge, with its dim lighting and plush furnishings, was far removed from her usual haunts. Not just because she'd had to make some physical concessions in order to avoid unwanted attention, grudgingly removing her piercings for the night and even temporarily coloring her hair a more traditional black. And not because she seemed at least half a century younger than most of the club's other members on show, dozing in chairs or over newspapers. No, the main reason Bex felt like a vegetarian at a pork butchers' convention was that she knew she was supposed to be "finding things out" but didn't really have the first idea of how to begin. She could roam the public spaces of the club at will. There were no age restrictions here: If you were rich enough to join, you were old enough to join. But she doubted she'd uncover any useful information in the lounges or at the bars or in the gym or anywhere like that. She had to get behind the scenes somehow.

She wished she had a partner. Even Eddie would be . . . Okay, so maybe not Eddie, but there were four other members of Bond Team she'd be happy to have with her right now.

Maybe she should sit down or something. Standing up in the middle of the Prescott Lounge, scratching her head and looking puzzled, like a contestant in a quiz show, was only likely to get herself noticed. "A good secret agent should blend in," she heard Senior Tutor Grant saying. That Japanese guy over by the table had had his eyes on her ever since she'd come in. Tall guy by Asian standards, Bex thought, hoping that wasn't being patronizing. Fortyish, maybe. And must work out: His dinner jacket barely concealed his bulging biceps. If he'd been twenty years younger . . . She grinned. The Japanese guy must have seen her. He turned away in disgust. His sense of propriety was obviously easily offended.

"Can I get you anything, Miss?" a polite waiter inquired at her side.

Okay, she'd better start secret-agenting. "No, thanks," she said, "I'm fine, although . . ."

"Yes, Miss?"

"I understand a friend of mine is working here at the moment. Well, a friend of a friend, actually. Name of Jarrett Jensen. Do you know where I might find him?"

"I'm afraid you must be mistaken, Miss," the polite waiter said. "Nobody by that name has ever been employed at the Centennial Club, as far as I am aware."

"Really?" Lie detection techniques. Look at the whole body, not just the face. Watch for that telltale physical sign of deceit. The slightest coloring of the cheek. The twitch of a muscle. A flutter of eyelids. "Are you sure?"

"I'm sorry, Miss. Please excuse me." A polite bow of the head and then she saw it. The waiter's eye. A nervous tic. He was lying.

Bex watched where he went. Over to the Japanese guy she'd observed before. So? Surely just asking if he wanted a drink. Seemed to be taking his time, though. Seemed to be saying a mouthful. Bex sat down at last, thought it best not to appear interested in other people's conversations, particularly when her ears were burning. But when she dared to glance that way again, the waiter had gone. The Japanese had not. And he was staring directly at her.

For a moment their eyes locked, and in that moment, Bex knew they were enemies. Then the man was turning on his heel and striding purposefully from the lounge.

She had to follow him. She didn't quite know why, but he was a lead. Bex, in turn, exited the lounge, glimpsed her quarry heading toward the restaurant. Maybe he'd got hungry all of a sudden.

She would have pursued him then. If hands hadn't suddenly gripped her shoulders. If a voice behind her hadn't suddenly said: "And where do you think you're going?"

She'd been cautioned, of course. Taking a SkyBike off school premise without permission. Taking *herself* off school premises without permission. Engaging in activity likely to endanger both herself and others — *without permission*. But Cally didn't care. She'd gone after Jensen for Mac, and she'd do the same again, with or without the system's blessing. A good secret agent knew how to improvise. Besides, she'd got results. And the bottom line was, in Spy High's line of work, results were all that mattered.

If only she could have gone with Bex, but until her teammate reported back from Centennial Club, there was nothing she could do to further the investigation. Except maybe one thing.

Cally sat in the IGC research suite sifting through the material Mac had downloaded on his final visit concerning the Temple of the Transformation. It simply defied belief that they were not involved in any way at all with the burning of the Refuge, not after what Mac had told her. The tapes made her angry. Guilty, too. She'd come away from the gathering feeling that the members of the Temple were a bunch of harmless losers. Watching video footage of them, she was beginning to change her mind.

One item in particular: a girl in her late teens, a pretty girl, whatever difference that made, smiling at the camera, her eyes wide with elation and her whole face suffused with joy. The caption along the bottom of the screen didn't seem to know whether she was called Alice or Rebecca: Both names appeared. "I've been so happy since I came to Temple Prime," she was declaring, "happier than I ever thought possible. My soul rejoices in the Temple and my spirit soars." She spoke them like words learned from a book. And behind the euphoria, if Cally could peel away the staring eyes, the flushed flesh, she suspected she'd find nothing but an empty hole, a deep, measureless void. "My life is now fulfilled," Alice/Rebecca was proclaiming, "and I look forward to my final Transformation." She was like a saint in rapture. "I wait only to be transformed."

Fair enough, Cally thought. But transformed into *what?*

"Ben!" Bex beamed, glad to see him. "You know how to make an entrance, don't you. What are you doing here?"

"I changed my mind." Ben's brow furrowed. "If there *is* anything dodgy going on at the club, which I doubt, I decided it'd be wiser for me to find out about it firsthand."

"I see you dressed for the occasion as well." Bex admired his tuxedo look, like James Bond at a casino.

"You, too," reciprocated Ben. "I almost didn't recognize you. Are those real pearls or Spy High issue?" He indicated her necklace.

"Let's hope you don't have to find out," Bex said. "Now come on. You've arrived just in time for the exciting part." She grabbed his hand and pulled him after her, almost immediately stopping again so Ben nearly fell over her.

"Bex, what —?"

At the end of the corridor, the Japanese man from the lounge was addressing the waiter she'd asked about Jarrett

Jensen in no uncertain terms. Bex doubted it concerned anything as mundane as bad service.

"There," she hissed to Ben. "Suspects numbers one and two. Quick, stand in front of me. If they look this way and recognize —"

"Suspected of what?" Ben tried to look nonchalant, nodding civilly to an elderly couple passing by on the way to the restaurant.

"Knowing Jensen and claiming not to. Quick!" Now Bex was yanking him backward. "He's coming."

They ducked into an alcove as the Japanese man glowered his way across the main reception area and up the central stairway, which for the lower floors of the building formed a perfect replica of the Centennial Club's original grand staircase. It made keeping him in sight while following at a safe distance childishly simple. Even Eddie could have managed it, Bex smirked.

Ben wasn't smirking. "Are you sure this guy's the real thing? He doesn't look very suspicious to me."

"The days when criminals prowled around in black-and-white-striped jerseys carrying sacks labeled 'swag' went out centuries ago, Ben," Bex retorted. They'd nearly reached the top of the staircase now. "So what's the deal? You don't trust my judgment?"

"I just don't want us jumping an entirely innocent president of some multinational company and getting sued for it."

"Listen," Bex said, "either we keep on his tail or we return to the Prescott Lounge and twiddle our thumbs with the over-nineties'-evening-out crowd. You're team leader, which do you want?"

"Okay," Ben conceded. "But you'd better be right."

"I love this job," grinned Bex. The pretense of periodic fittings ended with the final stair. Bex and Ben were now very much in the mid-twenty-first century, the décor minimalist and metallic. "And there goes our man." Disappearing down a minor corridor.

And "disappearing" was the word. The Bond Teamers peeked around the corner only to see . . . *nothing?* Bex couldn't believe her eyes. "But it's a dead end. Where did he go?"

Ben ventured into the corridor himself. "Well, either he's an expert in the art of invisibility," he mused, "or this end isn't quite as dead as we think."

"Does that mean something in English?" Bex said, joining him.

"You weren't with us when we had our first encounter with Dr. Frankenstein, were you, Bex?"

"Are you going somewhere with this, or are you just trying to put me in my place?"

"No, it's going somewhere," Ben assured her. "I think we're going somewhere. 'Cause I think the wall at the end of this corridor is just like one of the walls at Frankenstein's lodge." He reached out his hand. "Holographic." And his hand went through the wall. "Am I a genius or what?"

"I wouldn't applaud if I were you, though," warned a man's voice.

Bex groaned. "What is this? Do I have a sign on me saying 'creep up on this girl from behind' today?"

"If I were you, I'd put my hands in the air, very high, where I can see them, and I wouldn't make any sudden moves at all."

"Wouldn't you?" Ben said interestedly, turning slowly. "Why's that?"

"Because if you do, I'll put a hole in that nice frilly shirt you're wearing." It was the polite waiter, Bex recognized. Not so polite now, of course. Aiming a shock blaster at them probably meant he didn't have to be. "So hands up. Both of you."

"Do you think this is how he gets tips out of his customers?" Bex wondered idly, raising her hands as if it didn't matter. "And don't worry, Ben. I've got underarm protection."

"Shut up!" snapped the waiter. "Now you, too, boy. Up!"

"Boy?" Ben echoed. "Charming." He raised his hands, too, so the sleeves of his dinner jacket dropped back, exposing the cuffs of his shirt and their shiny gold links.

He made a sudden motion, too swift for the waiter to react. The cuff link spat sleepshot with perfect aim. The waiter wouldn't play any further part in the proceedings.

"Thought I should take a few precautions," Ben grinned at his partner.

"Sounds good to me." Bex rushed to the fallen waiter's side, retrieved his shock blaster. "And it'd be a shame to let this go to waste. Especially now that it proves I was right about our Japanese friend."

"Seems everyone was right about the Centennial Club," Ben admitted ruefully, "except me. Though lately, why should I be surprised?"

"Hey, don't worry about it," Bex said cheerfully. "We're all wrong once in a while. Saves us from being perfect. So when you walk through a holographic wall, does it make you sneeze or what?"

On the other side, set into the real wall, was an elevator door. Ben summoned the elevator itself. He was worried, and by more than his and Bex's immediate situation. How might whatever was going on at the Centennial Club reflect upon his own family and on Uncle Alex? Was something happening right under their noses? Luckily, he didn't have very long to dwell on such matters. The elevator was prompt. And empty. And it had only one button to press.

"Going up," announced Bex. "I wonder how far."

Ben tore off his bow tie and stuffed it in his jacket pocket. "Be ready for anything," he advised. "I mean *anything*."

The elevator came to a smooth stop. The two teenagers exchanged tense glances. The doors slid open.

Immediately they could see that they were on the periphery of a single large and open space. Its edges were in almost total darkness, always the secret agent's friend, the light source focused on the circular area in the center of the floor. The Japanese man stood in the light, and all around him were giant screens hanging from the ceiling. On all the screens that Ben and Bex could see from their limited perspective were faces — faces that were different and yet the same in one key respect.

"Man," Bex whispered. "These guys make the oldies downstairs look like children."

Age. On the faces on the screens, the decades could almost be counted in the deep cuts in the flesh, the parchment skin like ancient map markings for routes to forgotten cities, wrinkled like the heads had been badly stitched by blind seamstresses. Wisps of hair like grass in the desert. Weak, sunken eyes. Teeth, vampire white, that were not the same age as the rest of the body. Age. And plenty of it.

Around the perimeter of the lighted circle, there were banks of computers and other instrumentation. Things you could hide behind. Ben nodded toward them, and Bex took the hint. Front-row squats for whatever was about to unfold. In fact, if they'd just entered a movie theater, they'd have drawn disapproving glances from their fellow audience because the performance had already begun.

"Come now, gentlemen," their suspect was coaxing. Unlike downstairs, he seemed in good humor here. "These bids are neither a profitable use of my time nor yours, and excuse my impertinence in reminding you of the fact, but you have significantly less time to waste than I do."

"Business is business, Nagashima," croaked someone who resembled an Egyptian mummy without wrappings.

"And life is life, Mr. Baxenthorpe," responded the jovial Nagashima, "and life, remember, is what we are offering."

That was enough to render Mr. Baxenthorpe silent. Alongside him, however, a second face spoke up, this time in a French accent. "But if we pay the sum you are demanding, Nagashima, we must have guarantees on the efficacy and longevity of the treatment."

"Monsieur Foucault, gentlemen, what can I say?" protested Nagashima. "Let me repeat: Our operation at Temple Prime is running smoothly and efficiently. The benefits of the process are obviously clear to you. There remains a slight risk to the subject, yes, even though we are constantly refining our techniques, but you are all self-made men, you have all gone where others dared not to follow. What is life without risk? What have you got to lose?"

"You are correct, Nagashima," said Foucault. "I for one will meet your price. My doctors — these days I do not trust their smiles."

Delighted, Nagashima clapped his hands together and started to laugh. He didn't finish it. At that point the elevator doors opened again and several men, dressed as Centennial Club employees — waiter, barman, and chef — spilled out. All brandished shock blasters.

"Time to go," Ben decided.

"Shame. Just when I was getting comfortable. Oh, well," Bex lamented, and fired her own shock blaster.

The newcomers scattered in a spray of sparks, returning fire. The Bond Teamers retreated behind cover.

"What is going on here?" Nagashima demanded from center stage. Then he saw Bex. "You!" Cold rage flooded his features. He ran at her, scarcely seeming to register Ben.

Which gave him a chance to deploy his sleepshot. The cufflink spat. An easy shot, target advancing so making itself bigger all the time.

Nagashima dodged. Impossibly. With superhuman swiftness. The sleepshot projectile passed harmlessly by.

A less-adept secret agent than Ben might have let the shock of his opponent's agility delay his next move, but Ben knew that to survive in the field for long, you always had to have a plan B.

He sprang for Nagashima himself, at the last second diving low, sweeping with his legs together like he was break dancing, and taking the man's own legs out from under him. Both Nagashima and the computer into which he crashed would have had better days.

"Necklace!" Ben yelled. "Now!"

Bex plucked a pair of pearls from her necklace and tossed them toward the elevator. They shattered and billowed out dark, acrid smoke — smoke pellets, designed to deter pursuit and create confusion in enemy ranks. From the choking and coughing coming from the club's thugs, they were fulfilling their brief.

"Let's go!" Ben urged. "There's got to be another way out."

They darted between the screens where the circle of old men watched them with mingled outrage and astonishment. The excitement seemed to have been a little too much for Mr. Baxenthorpe, who appeared to be having a heart attack.

The Bond Teamers sped down a hopeful-looking corridor, aware that men with shock blasters were groping their way clear of the smoke and would be following very shortly. There was just enough time to reach what had to be a stairwell.

Kind of. But the steps led in one direction only: up.

"Not good," Ben muttered.

Bex peered upward. "Do we go back? Find another way?"

"Can't. They're behind us." Ben was already on the stairs, taking them three at a time. "We'll just have to find an elevator or something on the next floor up."

"Right." Bex paused, pulled another smoke pellet from her necklace and hurled it the way they'd come. "Might slow them down a bit," she muttered, then pounded after Ben.

A door was open at the top of the stairs. She felt colder air on her skin. Seemed this floor went in for air-conditioning in a big way. As soon as she made it to the door, she realized why.

They were on the roof.

"Ah, Ben, your idea about finding an elevator, I don't think it's going to happen. . . ."

No way down. Unwanted company about to put in an appearance. The Spy High manual probably had a word for situations like this.

Trapped.

CHAPTER SEVEN

"I guess if we both covered the door, we could maybe pick them off as they come through." It was the only plan under pressure that Bex could think of. "Ben? What do you . . . ? Ben?"

He wasn't there. Had obviously already dismissed defending the door as a viable option. Bex saw him standing on the very ledge of the roof, his back to her. He'd stripped off his jacket and seemed to be fumbling at the front of his trousers.

"Ben?" She ran toward him. "What are you doing? I know this is a tense moment but I hardly think you've got time to . . ."

He was peeling back the material of his cumberbund. Bex could make out coils of ultrathin cable wrapped around his waist. "Can't go up. Can't go down." An accurate summary of their position, Bex thought. "Gotta go sideways."

There was a towering office block alongside them. A sheer, unreachable office block.

"You want us to jump?" Bex gasped. "Er . . . I think I'll take my chances back there, thanks."

"Jump, no," grinned Ben, "but didn't you ever want to swing on a trapeze?"

He pressed a button concealed in his cumberbund. The cable shot across the gulf between the Centennial Club building and its neighbor, its velocity almost toppling Ben off the ledge. Bex held on to him like someone with a winning lottery ticket. The end of the cable struck the gleaming glass of the tower and stuck. Ben yanked on it to test its strength. He seemed satisfied.

"Treated with the same stuff that makes clingskin," he said. "We'll be perfectly safe." He pulled the cable taut.

"Safe for what?" wailed Bex, as if she didn't already know.

A shock blast sizzled the concrete to their left. Followed by yells for them to stay where they were.

Ben didn't think so. "Hold on tight," he warned. "Here we go."

She didn't want to scream really; it might give Ben the wrong impression. And he probably didn't want her screaming quite that close to his ear, either. But, when you were fifteen or twenty stories up, leaping into thin air with your arms wrapped around your team leader's neck and your legs around his waist, your continued health dependent on a length of string with delusions of grandeur, there were some things you just couldn't help doing. The wind slapped at her face like a nurse calming a hysteric. It was just as well; she hadn't eaten before she came out.

Bex and Ben plunged toward the office building.

"What? What?" She couldn't hear what he was shouting.

"Blast! The! Glass!" Then she could.

They were about to slam into the tower, red smudges to be soaped off by the window cleaner, unless . . . .

It was awkward to get a shot in, but Bex managed. The glass wall in front of them smithereened, vanished in a single explosive moment. The two teenagers swept through. Ben disengaged the cable, and they both tumbled forward across the floor, their training enabling them to control their fall, to roll with it, and to stand at the end with no bones broken.

They were in an office. So was a cleaner. The cleaner was pointing at them stupidly and moving his lips but no sound was emerging. His eyes bulged out so far it was almost possible to see behind them.

"Hi," said Bex. "We were just passing through. Thought we'd drop in."

Corporal Keene sat in the Committee Room at the Centennial Club and regarded its chairman coolly. So this was Alexander Cain. He'd been told of the man's relationship with Stanton, and he could already detect the source of some of Ben's arrogance and sense of superiority, those characteristics that Spy High training had been attempting to reduce in him. Keene came from a proud military family, was the latest in a long line of soldiers. He'd been raised to respect authority and to obey without question his superior officers. Alexander Cain, he believed, was a man who respected nothing and brooked no superior. Ben Stanton hadn't stood a chance.

"Well, I'm shocked, Mr. Keene."

"Agent Keene." The corporal wore no military uniform today. No true identity, either. As only an adult could interview Cain like this, it was a rare opportunity for Keene to go undercover.

"Agent Keene, of course. But it all sounds incredible. The Centennial Club employing known criminals? Acts of violence carried out within these walls? I know this is going to sound rather rude of me, but I find it impossible to believe you. I am not responsible for hiring and firing, as the phrase goes, but the person who is boasts the most respected credentials. We are extremely careful who works here. The club has a reputation to protect." Cain at last lifted his eyes to Keene's. They were piercing and powerful. "Might I ask how you came by this information?"

"We have our sources," Keene allowed. "Classified sources."

"Indeed," sniffed Alexander Cain. "Well, in this case, I fear they are mistaken." He stood up, impressive in his black suit.

"But as your agency considers these reports serious enough to warrant your present visit, naturally I will extend the club's full cooperation. We have nothing to hide."

"Thank you, Mr. Cain," said Keene.

"Now, while your colleague checks our records, perhaps you'd like me to escort you to the apparent location of last night's alleged incident. I only wish you could be a little more specific. . . ."

"Classified," said Keene.

"Of course," said Cain, with a smile that might also have been a sneer.

Keene followed him out of the Committee Room and up the central staircase, where the previous evening, according to their debrief mere hours ago, Stanton and Deveraux had rather more covertly pursued the man called Nagashima. Back at Spy High, calls had been made and the present inspection of the Centennial Club by Keene and a tech sanctioned via a legitimate government agency. The corporal didn't doubt for a second that his students had been telling the truth. Though not an imaginative man by nature, he suspected that there were elements at work within the Centennial Club, of which Alexander Cain knew nothing. Well, Mr. Chairman might just be in for a rude awakening.

". . . the quality of membership we have here attracts envy," Cain was explaining, "from those less blessed by the gods of success. I'm sure the sources in which you place such faith are simply mischief makers attempting to embarrass the club." He paused at the corner of a corridor. "After you, Agent Keene. A holographic wall, did you say?"

Stanton and Deveraux had said as much. But there was no

such thing now, and from the route they'd described, Cain had brought him to the right place. "Holograms can be switched off as well as on," Keene observed dryly. And there was an elevator at the end of the corridor.

Cain seemed to be struggling to understand the man's persistence. "Indeed," he conceded, "and if you wish to look for controls in the wall or wherever holograms are operated from . . ."

"I'd sooner see where this elevator goes, if that's all the same with you, Mr. Cain."

"Whatever you say, Agent Keene," sighed Alexander Cain. "But I can assure you, offices at the Centennial Club are the same as anywhere else."

Not these, Keene thought. *Not according to Stanton and Deveraux.* He pressed the single button. The elevator traveled upward. Last night the students had been in here, and their lives had been in jeopardy. Keene didn't like it when his students' lives were in jeopardy. He tensed himself for what he expected to be awaiting him on the other side of the elevator doors.

But when they opened, he still had to stifle a gasp of disbelief.

She only ever saw her parents in her dreams now. During the day, try as she might, she could no longer recall their faces, their voices, or even their names. It was as if her parents had been wiped clean from her conscious memory.

Yet at night, they came to her, in the quiet and the darkness of sleep. But they would persist in calling her by her old name, her dead name. She wasn't Alice now. The girl who'd been Alice had nothing to do with her. They would reach out to her as if to touch her with frail, forgotten fingers. They were reaching out to her now, as if to keep her with them.

But then Ruth woke her. "Rebecca." Speaking her true name. Her only name. "Rebecca, it's time." Ruth was smiling like an angel and garbed in the pure white robes of the Heavenly Host.

Rebecca felt strange, like she was floating, like she was awake but somehow the world around her was dreaming, its colors merging, its solids melting and becoming rain. She tried to tell Ruth. "I feel . . ."

Ruth already seemed to know. "It's time," she smiled. "You are to come with me, Rebecca. It's time for your final Transformation."

And Rebecca went with her, and they moved silently through the Temple, and it seemed as if they were entering heaven itself.

"Gabriel is waiting for you," Ruth said.

He was. He stood before them exuding light and peace. He put his hands on her head and he blessed her. She was in the Temple of Tranquillity, her drifting mind sensed that much at least, the holiest of holies. Something very special was about to happen, she knew that, too. There were shapes around her and they were moving.

"Daughter." Gabriel's voice was in her head. "Child of the Temple. Your moment has come, the time for your Transformation. You are blessed indeed."

Other hands were on her now, stronger hands, from sources she could not see.

"Gabriel?" And she wished she could remember her parents' faces.

"Have no fear," Gabriel soothed. "I will be with you." And then he said: "Put her in."

And now her hands seemed to be across her chest and something cold seemed to be pressing against her Temples and she didn't seem able to move. But why should she want to move, anyway? Why, when she was here with Gabriel? She saw him still, as if through glass, his generous features somehow distorted now, his smile seeming wider, more cruel. She seemed to see another with him, crookbacked and shriveled like he belonged in a grave. Momentarily, the thought chilled her, but then the thought was gone and Crookback was gone and Gabriel was gone, too. There was only herself.

Herself and the Transformation.

She felt it coming. Her flesh was tingling, and in her ears was a humming like the wings of angels beating against the sky. It was coming for her. Her heart was racing.

Oddly, now of all moments, she saw again her parents clearly, but now they no longer seemed to be reaching out for her. Their heads were bowed, their brows were beaten. They were turning, turning away.

And the tingling was sharper now, like needles pricking at her skin, all over her skin, and blood would gush from the tiny holes and blood was life.

They were leaving her. They were losing her. But Alice didn't want them to go. Not now. Not yet. She called to them. She cried out to them.

Then there was a howling in her ears, as though from fallen angels. The Transformation was upon her.

And it had all been going so well.

He and Bex had been greeted like conquering heroes upon their return to Spy High, battered and bruised, maybe, but essentially intact. Mission experience of any kind tended to impress. If Ben had wanted a first-year girl, now would have been a good time to make his move. But there was only one girl he wanted.

They'd been debriefed by Grant and Keene, checked over by the medics, and only then had they been allowed to rejoin their teammates.

"Some nasty bruises you've got there, Bex." Eddie.

"I'm afraid I've got them all over."

"Yeah? Can I see?"

Ben had expected Lori to approach him, had hoped that the danger he'd endured might remind her of her past feelings for him, but it had somehow been Cally, gazing at him with what could have been respect. "You went after all," she acknowledged. "After all you said about your family and the club, you still put the team first. You might have helped us find the people behind Mac's death, Ben. Thank you." And then she touched his hand, lightly, a little like the way Lori had used to do.

Lori . . . He sought her out himself. And that was when everything started to go wrong.

"Back in one piece, then," she said.

"As always. Thought you might have come over for a closer look."

"Thought you might have misinterpreted it if I did."

"How is it possible to misinterpret concern for a teammate?"

"By reading concern as something more. By thinking boyfriend-girlfriend instead of teammates. Ben," and he'd known what she was going to say and she didn't need to say it, "I'll always care for you, I want you to know that, but if you're thinking there's a chance of us getting back together, don't. There isn't. We can't give each other what we want in a relationship. I'm sorry."

Not as sorry as Daly's going to be, he thought.

But the final straw hadn't been Lori and Jake. It had been Grant. When later that night he and Bex had been summoned back to the senior tutor's study, Ben had assumed congratulations would be in order, at the very least that they'd learn what Keene's visit to the Centennial Club had unearthed.

"Nothing."

"Beg your pardon, sir," Bex had frowned. "Is that nothing as in not a thing, zilch, nada, drawn a blank?"

"Your ability to understand everyday English is laudable, Bex," Grant had replied. "And you are quite correct. No holographic wall. No circle of screens — the floor where you claim you saw them contains nothing more sinister than office workers at their desks. No Mr. Nagashima on any membership list. No record now of even Jarrett Jensen ever having worked there."

"Nagashima must have changed everything, covered his tracks." Ben had been quick to protest. "What, you think we made the whole thing up? There's still a hole in the building next door, isn't there? And we've got a file that *proves* Jensen was an employee."

Bex had pitched in, too. "And what he said about Temple Prime. Shows a link with the Temple of the Transformation, just like Cally claimed."

"Speculation," Grant had said. "Supposition. Gossip. Of course I believe you. So does Corporal Keene, but whoever this Nagashima person is, he's clever. Computer files can be faked one way or another, so our evidence as to Jarrett Jensen's time at the club is not particularly convincing."

"So is that it?" Ben had marveled incredulously. "Case closed?"

"Case paused," Grant had adjusted. "Mr. Deveraux agrees that we should now carry out routine surveillance on both the Centennial Club and the Temple of the Transformation, but that until any concrete evidence arises of illegal activity on the part of either organization, we do nothing more. That is all."

Ben stalked from Grant's study feeling bitterness and rage inside him. He ignored Bex's invitation for a coffee in the rec room, preferring to be on his own — without Lori. He'd have to get used to it.

Outside the school, the night seemed bleak and lonely. "Snap," scowled Ben.

The next day he videophoned Uncle Alex. He had no choice in the matter. But he would have to choose his words as carefully as a politician during an interview. Even the slightest nudge-nudge, wink-wink, Deveraux-Academy-is-more-than-you-think-style hint as to Spy High's existence to anyone not actively involved in its work, and he might as well book an appointment at the mind-wiping clinic at the same time. But he couldn't simply ignore his loyalty to Uncle Alex, either. He had to know from someone he trusted that there was something amiss at the Centennial Club. He had to be warned.

"Ben," greeted Uncle Alex from the screen, "what a pleasant surprise."

"Yeah, Uncle Alex. You okay?"

"I'm well, thank you. And how are you? And more important, perhaps, how is the lovely Lori?"

"Ah, yeah. Lori." Not an auspicious start to the call. But Ben could scarcely lie to Uncle Alex. "Actually, I have no idea. The thing is, Uncle Alex, uh, I've split up with Lori."

"Really? I *am* surprised. Such a delightful girl."

"Yeah, well, we just . . ." He thought it best not to mention what Lori had said about *him.* "What do they call it in divorce-speak? Irreconcilable differences? Yeah, I think we had some of those."

"Not concerning that black-haired boy, I hope," said Uncle Alex.

"Jake? Uh, why do you say that?"

"Because there is only one course of action to take when faced by a rival in love," assured Uncle Alex, "and that is to remove the rival. Never let anyone come between you and your desires, Ben. Remember the cliff. Claim the sky for yourself."

"Yeah, thanks, Uncle Alex, I'll . . . Uncle Alex, there's something I need to talk to you about. It's about the Centennial Club."

"The club?" Rarely for Uncle Alex, he seemed genuinely caught off guard.

"Two nights ago, I was there. With a friend."

"Yes? You're a member, Ben." Uncle Alex's eyes narrowed. "I assume your friend is, too."

"We probably went where we shouldn't have. We were probably in the wrong to start with. But we were chased by men with guns, men who seemed to be working at the club."

"Chased? Men with guns?" Checking he'd heard right. "Is this some sort of joke, Ben? If so, I am not finding it amusing. Yours is the second . . ." A pause, then understanding. "Did you report this to the authorities? Because we had a very strange visit at the club yesterday, representatives from some sort of government agency." Another pause. "You don't know anything about that, do you, Ben? That isn't why you're calling me now, is it?"

"I can't say, Uncle Alex. I shouldn't even be talking to you about this." Voice urgent, pleading. "But you've just got to believe me. Trust me. Something's going on at the club. You need to be careful."

"Oh, I am," said Uncle Alex, his composure quickly regained.

"But . . ." Ben was about to say more when Jake Daly entered the room.

"Not interrupting anything, am I?" He crossed to his bed.

Ben glowered. Daly's whole life was an interruption. "I've got to go, Uncle Alex. Think about . . . you know. I'll speak to you soon."

"You do that, Ben, and I'll bear in mind what you've said." Uncle Alex leaned forward to turn the videophone off. "Oh, and Ben. You take care, too."

"Was that your Uncle Alex?" Jake asked as he rummaged through the drawer of his bedside table.

"What's it got to do with you?" Ben snapped. He hoped Jake hadn't heard anything of their conversation, or with a word to Grant, Jake could be the one removing the rival.

"Just being friendly, that's all."

"Well, I'm sure there are others more receptive to your friendliness than me," Ben smarted. He knew of one, at least.

"Look, Ben." Jake was conciliatory. "I know you're mad because of Lori and you. . . . I can understand that. I guess I'd feel the same." *Only you don't have to.* Ben was seething. And was Jake about to reveal his own relationship with Lori? "You might not believe this, but I'm sorry things didn't work out." Jake was right. He didn't believe that. "But you can't keep dwelling on it. Lori's moving on. You're going to have to move on, too. You let this get to you, and you'll end up choking on your own bitterness."

"Well, thanks for the homespun country wisdom, Jake," Ben said, "but you don't need to worry. I'm not going to let myself dwell on mine and Lori's breakup. I'm going to be doing something about it. Real soon."

Either Nagashima was in the habit of talking to himself or he was communicating with someone not in the room via a concealed mike and an earpiece. The latter seemed more probable.

"Not even a setback," he was scorning. "A minor relocation, nothing more. Our program does not even have to pause. It has been said that the eyes of the authorities are always blind. Let the deception continue."

He prowled the floor restlessly, evidently finding it tedious to tolerate the voice of his interlocutor. Until he suddenly stopped dead and a sadistic smile lit up his face.

"Indeed? Now that *is* interesting. And you don't wish to deal with the matter yourself? Oh, I quite understand. No, of course. I would consider it an honor."

He moved to the center of the room, where a steel railing hooped an empty space in which a man might stand. He activated a switch on the railing. The floor within its bounds opened wide like a mouth about to scream. From below, a suit of golden and metal armor rose up to display itself before Nagashima.

"No," he said. "No need. In my country, we have a saying: The true warrior fights alone. I have something in mind that I am certain will please you."

Lovingly, Nagashima stroked the armor's winged helmet, its visor and neck protector, the plated shoulder guards, the steel corselet to defend the chest. The armor of a samurai warrior, scarcely altered over the centuries. And then he came to the gauntlets, the intricate web of wires like veins, the complex circuitry woven into the palms, the fingers ringed like dynamos. Some aspects of the armor, it seemed, *had* moved with the times.

"The boy will die," announced Nagashima coldly. "The psimurai will kill him."

CHAPTER EIGHT

Jake wasn't big on pretenses, however well-intentioned they might be. His general policy was to tell it like it was and take the consequences, a far safer bet in the long run. So his own feeling, particularly after his brief exchange with Ben the other day, was that he and Lori should tell everyone immediately that they *were* he and Lori. It would prevent Ben from trying to rekindle a flame that was now ashes. It might help him get on with his life instead of moping around all the time and biting people's heads off whenever they asked him something. It would certainly render unnecessary Lori having to leave him notes like the one presently in his pocket: "Jake. Hologym. ASAP. Lori." He wondered with amusement whether she intended him to eat the piece of paper later to stop it from falling into enemy hands. Anyone would think they were playing around as secret agents. Ridiculous.

But he didn't waste any time getting to the hologym.

Maybe he'd been too prompt. The place looked deserted. No blonde bombshell. Nobody at all. "Lori?" Maybe she was hiding behind the row of spare shock suits and holohelmets. "Are you there?"

There was a movement at the door behind him. Jake turned, expecting to want to smile. Instead, his lips remained glued steadfastly together.

"Looking for someone, Jake?" Ben was grinning nonchalantly. He'd closed the door. "Only I'm afraid Lori can't make it. Will I do?"

"What are you talking about?" Jake probed suspiciously. "How'd you know I was meeting Lori here?"

"Jake. Hologym. ASAP." Ben was holding a computer disk in his hand. He slotted it into the hologym door's locking mechanism.

"You read Lori's note?"

"Not quite. I wrote it." Ben considered. "So whether that makes it Lori's note or not I'm not sure." He removed the disk from the lock and patted it like a pet.

"What did you just do, Ben?" *We should have told him sooner,* he repeated to himself.

"What, with this?" The disk. "This is a kind of variation on Cally's chameleon unit. I fooled the lock into thinking it was receiving a signal from the control room. I've locked us in."

"Mind telling me why, Ben? Not often you're so eager for my company you don't give me a chance to leave."

"I thought it was time we had a talk."

"Yeah? Any subject in particular?"

"I think you know what subject in particular. My girlfriend."

"She's not your girlfriend. Not anymore."

"Not since you stole her from me, Jake."

"I didn't *steal* anyone." Jake felt his indignation rising. "Lori isn't a thing, an object that can be stolen, given, taken. She makes her own decisions. She makes her own choices. And she's chosen me, Ben. You've got no right to complain. You had your chance, and you blew it. How did you find out about us, anyway?"

"Because I'm a spy. Because I'm team leader. What does it matter? You're messing with my girl, Daly, and I want it to stop. Lori'll get back together with me if you just fade away quietly."

"You're deluding yourself, Stanton," scoffed Jake, "but why

should that surprise me? You've had a lot of practice. And I'm not fading away quietly, loudly, or any other way, just so you're sure. What I am doing, though, is walking out of here, so if you'd kindly just *un*lock us."

"Can't." Ben waved the disk at Jake. "If you want this, you'll have to fight me for it."

"You're kidding, right?"

"Wrong." Ben crossed to the holohelmets, removed one from its hanger. "Come to think of it, why don't you fight me for Lori as well?" He threw the helmet at Jake's head. Jake caught it in front of his face like a football. "Nice reflexes."

"Stanton," Jake said, "you don't need Lori. You need help. I'm not fighting you for anything."

"Why not? Scared you'll lose? Don't think Lo's important enough? That's not a good sign for your continued relationship — maybe you should give it up now." Ben sneered. "Or maybe you're just like all those other Domers, too afraid to take a risk, hiding away from the Big Bad World behind a shield of glass and steel? Maybe you shouldn't even be at Spy High at all, Jake, what do you think?" If that didn't anger Jake to action, Ben thought, nothing would.

Jake shook his head wearily. "All right, Ben, if a fight's what you want, if that's what it'll take to restore your obviously flagging self-esteem, I'll take you on. But I'm telling you now, it won't prove anything."

"We'll see," said Ben. "Change."

Silently, swiftly, they stripped off their normal clothes and climbed into shock suits, fixed on and made comfortable their holohelmets. He'd had this coming for a long time, Ben was thinking. Time to put Daly in his place, just as Uncle Alex had recommended. And Jake shared a similar view, though in reverse: Stanton had always been so superior, so sure of himself. There had been tensions between them since day one. Maybe now they'd finally get things sorted, and if that meant taking Ben down a peg or ten, Jake was just the spy to do it.

"Activate duel program." Ben spoke into his helmet's communicator.

"Voice pattern recognized," the system spoke back. "Which dueling scenario would you like today, Student Stanton?"

"Pistols at dawn?" grunted Jake.

"Voice pattern recognized," said the computer. "Student Daly selects pistols at —"

"No, computer," Ben interrupted sharply. "Selection overridden. Let's have something requiring a little more skill. Selection: swords. Subsection: rapiers. Begin."

At once, their vision controlled by the holohelmets, the boys saw that they were clutching rapiers in their right hands, the blades long, thin, and very deadly. If they were real, of course. The gym's safety protocols meant that the helmet's input to the brain always reminded that organ that the weapons in use were holographic and that any injuries incurred during combat were only illusory.

Ben's venom, however, was one hundred percent authentic. "En garde!" he yelled, and thrust his rapier forward.

Jake deflected the attack, sidestepping neatly. "You'll have to be quicker than that," he advised.

"Don't worry," Ben gritted. "I will be."

He lashed out again, his blade slicing the air with stinging speed. Jake was on the defensive, a relentless rain of blows from Ben restricting his movements to blocks and parries only, and always he was retreating. Ben's assault seemed wild, but his control of his sword was consummate, instinctive. His fury was inspiring him. "I'm going to cut you down to size, Daly," he muttered. "Literally."

And Jake was too slow. Fending off a hack at the head left his torso vulnerable. Ben's rapier slashed at his side, stabbed through shock suit, through skin. At least, according to his holohelmet it did. In reality . . .

Jake gasped, doubled up in sudden agony. His left side, his apparently wounded side, it was burning, a level of pain not normal for a routine combat program. Something was wrong.

"Hurts, doesn't it?" Ben didn't sound overly sympathetic. "That's because I disengaged the safety protocols before we started. Thought it might focus our minds."

"Stanton," Jake winced, as he tried to keep the pain inside him, "you're mad."

"Is that Daly-speak for 'I surrender'?"

"It is not!"

Jake lunged to his feet again, swiping at Ben but signaling his intention far too early. Again, a lightning counterattack forced him to back off, to block, to parry. Sooner or later, Ben would breach his defenses. Stanton had probably been dueling when normal kids were climbing trees or playing ball. Jake might as well be honest and admit that he was no match for his opponent in terms of skill. In terms of cunning, however . . . If Ben's technique was not a weakness, his arrogance always was.

No further attempt to stand his ground. Jake stumbled backward awkwardly, clumsily, earning a shout of laughter from Ben, who surged forward with even greater verve. He couldn't lose now. Daly was there for the taking. His sword arm was dropping, his whole body sagging. He was beaten. In a second, he'd have the tip of his sword at Daly's throat.

But in that second, like a cobra striking from nowhere, Jake's rapier flashed. Unexpectedly. Unbelievably. Ben lost the grip on his own weapon. It clattered to the floor.

The tip of Jake's sword was at his throat.

"Wha —?"

"Is that Stanton-speak for 'I surrender'?"

"You won." Ben struggled to comprehend the fact. "You beat me."

"No, Ben," corrected Jake, almost with pity. "You beat yourself. As usual."

As if by magic, Jake's rapier vanished.

"Dueling program terminated manually," advised the computer. "Good day, Corporal Keene."

"For some it might be." Jake and Ben heard Keene's voice now over their communicators. They didn't need to see him to realize he was not happy. "But not for everyone. Perhaps you'd be good enough to remove those shock suits, Stanton, Daly. Then perhaps you'd be good enough to unlock the hologym door. And *then*, I think it would be best if we paid a visit to Senior Tutor Grant."

"Outrageous," Grant emphasized, as if someone in his study might be tempted to disagree with him. Bearing in mind the only candidates were a stone-faced Corporal Keene or Ben and Jake, both with heads hanging, that possibility seemed unlikely. "Overriding the security functions of the hologym door? Disengaging the safety protocols of the combat programs? Risking potentially serious neural damage to you both? And all because of some petty, paltry feud? You're training to be secret agents here, let me remind you, not prima donnas. I thought your differences had been worked out last year. It is deeply disturbing to me to discover otherwise."

"I'm sorry, sir." Ben felt the inadequacy of his response.

So did the senior tutor. "After our previous interview, Ben, I'm afraid 'sorry' is simply a word. I'd have expected better from a student of your pedigree."

"It wasn't Ben's fault, sir," Jake found himself intervening. He wasn't quite sure why. "It was mine. I goaded him into the fight."

Ben looked at Jake quizzically. "That's not true, sir. And I can't let Jake take any of the blame for something that was entirely my responsibility."

"I'm pleased to hear that, at least," Grant acknowledged. "Taking full responsibility for one's actions is one of the first qualities of leadership. Unfortunately, Ben, it has come a little too late for you." Ben's eyes widened in alarm. "Under the circumstances, given this reckless and irresponsible behavior, only one punishment seems appropriate. . . .

"You're kidding, Jake, right? Tell me you're kidding?" Eddie was astonished.

"Removed from the leadership of Bond Team," repeated Lori, like she was reading the obituary of someone she'd once known. "That's terrible."

"Bit of a downer, yeah," opined Bex.

"Poor Ben," mused Cally.

Jake had called his fellow team members together in one of the classrooms to break the news before Grant did it officially. A classroom was a little more private than the rec room.

"Poor Ben?" Lori echoed. "Worse than that. This'll destroy him. Team leader's everything he wanted to be. He needed that recognition." And she was thinking, *First I leave him, then he loses the leadership. Were the two connected?* She felt the first troubling stirrings of guilt.

"So what happened to you, Jake?" Cally asked.

"Oh, nothing," Jake shrugged. "Demerits, temporary removal of privileges. Nothing like Ben."

"What I want to know," began Eddie, whose thirst for knowledge was not legendary, "is why Ben was picking a fight with you in the first place, Jake? I mean, what had you done? Slurred the Stanton name or something?"

Jake hesitated, glanced at Lori, decided anyway. He wasn't big on pretenses. "I'm seeing Lori and Ben found out."

A trio of amazed faces. "Is it true, Lori?" Bex spoke for them all.

Lori nodded, her heart sinking. So she *was* to blame. It was all her fault. And yet she knew she'd been *right* to break up with Ben, *right* to take up with Jake. Why couldn't things just be left at that? Why did they always have to be so complicated?

"We were going to tell you," Jake said. "We were waiting for the right time."

"Ah, timing," said Eddie. "The secret of good comedy. Don't ever go into comedy, Jake."

"Well, I think the two of you'll look good together," approved Bex. "Suited. Kind of like Romeo and Juliet. Bonnie and —"

"Don't go there again, Bex, not right now," Lori smiled wanly.

"Yeah," said Eddie. "Congratulations." So Ben and Jake had both scored big since they'd been at Spy High. How come the unique Nelligan charm still wasn't off the mark? He glanced Bex-ward. Chance would be a fine thing. . . .

"So what happens now?" Cally asked.

"I guess we get to elect a new team leader," supposed Jake.

"I didn't mean that," said Cally. "I meant Ben. Lori's right. He's got to be devastated. What are we going to do about Ben?"

It was no good. With his life crashing down around him, he couldn't keep up the self-contained, self-sufficient, nothing-I-can't-handle façade any longer. Not even the Stantons were superhuman. He had to talk to someone.

Only question was, who? Lori would have been the obvious choice, once, when he meant something to her. Jake? Hardly. The others? He'd never really been close to any of his teammates (and whose fault was *that*? a small voice was asking). Clearly, Grant or Keene were out. There was only one person Ben knew he could turn to, one person he could trust, who'd know what he should do.

But Uncle Alex wasn't there. Away on business, his butler said. Scheduled to be back tomorrow, and in the meantime could not be contacted under any circumstances.

So that was it. Ben was on his own. He'd finally succeeded in standing apart from the others. How did it feel?

It was a feeling Ben wanted to run away from (but Stantons didn't run from anything, did they?). He grabbed a jacket and was out the door.

As was the rest of Bond Team.

"What's this?" he said defensively. "A deputation? Funeral party? Come for a bit of a laugh — how-the-mighty-have-fallen kind of thing?"

"Of course not, Ben," said Lori, hurt at the insinuation. "We want to say how sorry we are. . . ."

"Oh, yeah." Ben laughed bitterly. "That's really convincing coming from you, Lori."

"Ben," sighed Jake, "don't you ever *learn*?"

"Well, I'm sorry, too. Sorry that I won't be hanging around to become the object of your sympathies. Keep the bedside manners and pained expressions for someone who needs them. I'm out of here." He stalked off down the corridor.

"Ben," Lori called after him, "where are you going?"

He called back, "As if you care!"

The increased leisure time promised at the dawn of the computer age, machines to perform mundane tasks, robots to run the world while humans frolicked in a kind of endless summer, had never come to pass. Rather than liberating them from their labor, computers had opened the way for people to do more in the same amount of time. They'd also threatened job security and so made the workforce less likely to resist increases in its hours or in the number of tasks it was instructed to carry out. Truth be told, the worker in the mid-twenty-first century slaved harder and for longer than his or her counterpart in the late twentieth. Leisure opportunities were limited, so people needed to make the most of them.

A favorite destination was the Pleasure Malls, where the good times rolled forever and where work really was a four-letter word never to be mentioned. A 24-7 drug, sanctioned by the government, to lull the population into forgetting its problems, at least for as long as it could afford to stay there.

It was Ben's first and only port of call in his retreat from Spy High.

And maybe a wrong one. The shrieks and squeals from the excited throng jostling him on every side stabbed at his ears like daggers. The faces contorted in manic merriment, he wanted to be one of them, but it would all be so false, so meaningless. Like the pictures of paradise that writhed ever changing on the walls, the ceilings, the floor, making the partygoers feel that they were walking on air. Unreal.

He decided to find a club or a disco, somewhere he could hide in the music and not come out. There were plenty to choose from that allowed entry for teenagers: soul, urban, dance, moon mood, cyberblues, neutronic.

Ben took the first available option. A sad song was playing, which was just what he needed right now, the opportunity to *wallow*. The place wasn't too crowded, either. Ben found a booth and sat in it. Planned on sitting there for quite a while.

"And she ain't coming back. No, she ain't coming back. . . . And I'm down on the floor, and I can't take no more. . . ."

Ben knew where the singer was coming from. He found himself almost by accident watching a couple dancing. They were maybe a year or so older than him. The girl was pretty, had Lori's long blonde hair. Looked a bit like Lori, actually.

". . . 'Cause she ain't coming back . . ."

And she didn't seem to be having much fun. Her partner's dancing was so leaden that he seemed barely able to move his legs. The girl's gaze was wandering: It drifted to Ben. It caught his eye. She knew he was watching her. She smiled.

Ben thought he'd do the girl a favor.

"Excuse me." He'd got up and was tapping the boy on the shoulder almost before he realized it. If Lori didn't want him, there were other girls that would. Had she heard the one about fish in the sea? "Excuse me. I'd like to cut in."

"What?" The boy peered at him with irritation. "Get lost, blondie. Find your own girl."

"I have," said Ben, "only right now she happens to be dancing with you."

And what girl wouldn't want two boys fighting over her? Ben thought bleakly. Actually, he knew of one.

"Look. I told you to get lost. Do I have to make you as well?"

"You can try," said Ben.

The boy did. He threw a punch, probably what he imagined was quickly. He was like slow motion to Ben, who dodged to the side. Seized the arm as its momentum carried it through. Twisted it around and up behind the boy's back. Exerted pressure.

"What was that about getting lost?"

"Aagh! Aagh! You're breaking . . . aagh!"

And the girl wasn't screaming at him to stop or anything.

"Who's getting lost? Who is?"

"I am . . . aagh! I am . . ."

"Good," said Ben, "so do it now."

He shoved the boy away from him, watched him hurry into the depths of the club cradling his wrenched arm, noticed that he didn't even glance toward his former partner.

"Wow, that was amazing," the girl was admiring.

"It was, wasn't it," Ben said hollowly. The blonde was pressing up close to him, almost against him, and there was too much red on her lips and too much black around her eyes, and at this distance she didn't look like Lori at all.

Ben was ashamed.

"Kenny works out and everything," the blonde girl was saying. "You must be really strong. I like boys who are really strong. I'm Brandy."

Somehow, Ben didn't want to tell her who he was. He shouldn't have done what he just did. He shouldn't even be here.

Maybe the girl could read his thoughts. She suddenly gasped, took a step backward. But she wasn't even looking at him now. She was looking past him.

Ben turned. Maybe Kenny was on the comeback trail with his other arm. But it wasn't Kenny.

It was a samurai warrior.

CHAPTER NINE

Ben's first thought was that the man in the samurai armor must be a member of the Pleasure Mall's staff. The traditional iron mask, the *men*, completely concealed the newcomer's face, so Ben couldn't tell whether he was smiling insanely, in common with the mall's other employees, or not. "Aren't you in the wrong place?" he said. "The sushi bar's on the restaurant floor."

"I am in the right place." The warrior's voice seemed as cold and inflexible as the metal through which it issued. "I am your death."

"Say that again?" Obviously not an employee, then, or at least one who wasn't dependant on the hourly wages. Killing customers tended to be bad for a career. But Ben could still hardly take the threat seriously. "Is this part of the entertainment or what?" Some of his fellow revelers were circling around him and the samurai, laughing, pointing at the gleaming golden armor, applauding.

The warrior crossed his arms over his chest, bowed slightly. "If you do not resist, it will all be over very quickly for you."

But what if it wasn't a gag? The club's heat, its noise, the riotous clamor of its patrons — they were confusing Ben, making it hard to think. What was he doing just standing there?

The samurai stretched out his arms like he was being crucified. The golden wings on either side of his helmet, adjacent to his Temples, began to hum as though a current was being newly generated. They turned a pale yellow. They turned white, glowing, brilliant.

"What is this?" Ben questioned, tensing instinctively. "Who are you?"

And the samurai's gauntlets were blazing now, like fists of fire. And then, with an electric crackle, the shape of a sword sprouted from each hand, silhouettes in flaming white. The *kitana*, the long curved blade of the samurai, in the right hand; the shorter but no less deadly *wakizashi* in the left. Ben recognized them from martial arts lessons: the large and the small, the *daisho* weaponry of Japan's mightiest warriors.

He knew the man in the armor after all. "Nagashima."

The kitana swept down upon him like an executioner's ax. Ben threw himself backward, beyond the range of its sizzling arc. He collided with Brandy, with others whose amusement with what was happening was now beginning to falter. The psimurai — a samurai powered with psionic energy — advanced toward him.

"Get out of here!" Ben cried. "Call security!"

The kitana and the wakizashi flashed in tandem. Ben felt their heat as they almost grazed his flesh, but he ducked low, dived to the right, rolled, crouched for a counterattack. Some of the dancers now darted for the door. Shrieks of laughter turned to shrieks of fear.

More room to maneuver, Ben was judging. Whatever else, he had to stay out of reach of those swords. Not steel, clearly, but psionic, operated by the power of thought. Well, maybe he ought to give Nagashima something else to think about.

Ben grabbed a chair by its legs, swung it up and charged. The kitana sliced it in two.

The follow-up with the wakizashi might have done the same for Ben, but if one move fails, work it into the next. In battle, never pause. In combat, always seek the offensive.

Ben kept his momentum, barreled into Nagashima low, like a bowling ball. Strike one! The psimurai went down. Ben's chance. If he could twist the man's helmet off, break the connection between the wings and the gauntlets . . . But Nagashima was alert to the danger. The kitana scorched through the air, forced Ben back. And now there was little scope for attack. The psimurai was on his feet, closing in. The twin swords burned with psionic energy.

"If you know any prayers, boy," Nagashima found time to gloat, "repeat them now."

That gloating time: an agent in the field could always rely on it. It was an integral part of the megalomaniac's psychology, they'd been taught — the need to boast. The need to brag. The need to wallow publicly in their triumphs. One theory was that it was compensation for a lack of parental attention during childhood. Right at the moment, though, Ben couldn't care less about theory. Survival was a rather more practical business. And gloating time meant that Nagashima hadn't simply pressed ahead with his advantage and put an end to Benjamin T. Stanton Jr. Instead, he'd paused.

And a chair made a direct hit on the side of his helmet. For a second, the power source in the wings flickered. The daisho paled. Ben rammed into Nagashima, fists flailing, beating him back even through the protective armor.

Whoever had thrown that chair, Ben owed them his life.

He'd better not waste it. Nagashima was recovering from the initial shock. The swords were crackling with renewed power.

"Time to go, Ben."

His thoughts entirely, but who . . . ?

It was Cally. Cally was at the door.

"What?"

"Later. Move!"

They were out into the corridor. Security guards were running toward the club, armed with regulation issue shock blasters but not looking exactly in tip-top physical condition to face the psimurai. Nagashima mocked as he too emerged: "Go home to your wives. This is no concern of yours."

"You kids get behind us," recommended a plump-faced security guard whose recent exertions had brought a reddish tinge to his cheeks. "We'll take care of this."

"I doubt it," muttered Ben.

The guards opened fire on Nagashima nonetheless. Their shock blasts sparked uselessly off his armor. It was to their credit that they edged closer rather than farther away.

"Cal, what are you doing here? Are the others with you?"

"Reinforcements of one only. Sorry."

"Sorry nothing. Are you packing? Sleepshot? Blasters? Anything?"

"Negative. I wasn't expecting to find this kind of a party."

"You and me both, Cal."

"So what do we do?" After everything that had gone on lately, Cally was still asking *him* what they should do? "Any chance of taking this guy out with just the two of us and no weapons?"

The plump-faced security guard wasn't making recommendations now. It was all he and his colleagues could do to keep clear of the psimurai's swords. One wrong move and it wouldn't be just his cheeks that were red.

"These guys are going to get slaughtered," predicted Ben. "We've got to do something. And you're forgetting, Cal, we've always got one weapon with us. Our brains. And I've an idea." He quickly outlined his plan.

By now, the security guards were in retreat, anyway. When the two strangely intense kids that the psycho in the armor seemed to be targeting shouted at them — and in voices that seemed used to authority — to fall back, nobody had the strength to argue. The corridor was cleared. Nobody and nothing between the psimurai and the two Bond Teamers.

"It had been intended for me to eliminate only you," Nagashima addressed Ben, "but your friend I will accept as a bonus." The daisho blazed.

"That's real generous of you," nodded Cally, bracing herself.

"Let's show you how much we appreciate it." Ben's voice was icy with purpose. "Now, Cal!"

They raced at Nagashima side by side. Ridiculing their impudence, the psimurai extended both arms. The wakizashi would be sufficient for the girl. The kitana he would reserve for the boy. They were flinging themselves toward suicide. Together they would . . .

. . . part. They parted. Ben went right. Cally, left. The daisho slashed, but Nagashima had underestimated the speed of his opponents' reflexes, and their courage. Cally clenched her arms around his wakizashi arm. Ben seized the other. Nagashima struggled to shake them off but they seemed locked to him, each holding on and preventing his blades from being a threat to their partner. Worse, now he could see what they intended. They were forcing his daisho together. They were going to use his own weaponry against him. And if the two psi-powered swords should meet . . .

Psionic overload. The flash as the blades shorted out was

blindingly bright, the energy feedback jolting Ben and Cally to the floor as if they'd suffered an electric shock. A minor electric shock. They were on their feet again in seconds.

The same could not be said for the psimurai. The golden armor was blackened and smoldering. The gauntlets were cracked and blistered on the hands. The helmet held no fire.

Cally was there at once, loosening the neck protector, feeling for a pulse. She remembered doing much the same thing with Mac not so many nights ago. Then she'd found a pulse. Not this time. "He's dead, Ben."

"Yeah?" Ben massaged his shoulder. "Better him than us, Cal. Not that I expected *such* an extreme reaction . . . Help me get his helmet and mask off."

"Any idea who this guy is?" Cally worked at the *men.* "And why he wanted to kill you?"

"Yes and yes," said Ben grimly. "*How* he found me I don't know, but this is the guy Bex and I saw at the Centennial Club." As Cally stripped the mask from the face. "Cal, meet Mr. Nagashima."

Cally stared at the psimurai in bafflement, returned her gaze to Ben. "Are you sure?"

"I don't understand." With equal mystification. "What's going on?"

The man in the armor was Asian, all right. But he also had to be at least eighty years old.

It was remarkable how useful top-grade security clearance could be. A quick retina scan to establish their credentials and the manager of the Pleasure Mall was moving out of his office while Ben and Cally were moving in, at least until Corporal Keene arrived to take both them and the body of the psimurai back to Deveraux.

Ben was pacing the room, brow furrowed like a recently ploughed field and still not understanding. "I mean, it *had* to be Nagashima, the Japanese motifs and everything. I mean, who else has got it in for me right now?" He saw Cally raising her eyebrows. "Oh, thanks. What? You mean there's a line?"

"I mean we *do* still have enemies out there. Vlad Tepesch for one."

"True, but this doesn't seem quite his style," doubted Ben. "There's not much evidence of samurai warriors in Wallachian culture. But whoever he is, how do you explain the guy's *age*? How could someone who possibly can't even chew his own food fight like that? I didn't see any signs of rheumatism or arthritis, did you?"

"The techs'll sort it when we reach Spy High," said Cally.

"I guess so." Which brought Ben to his next issue of concern. "By the way, Cal, thanks for being here. Without you, I don't know what might have happened. The psimurai was backing me into a corner, pretty much literally."

"You'd have found a way to beat him." Cally seemed confident.

"Maybe. But what I wanted to ask then I'll ask now. What *are* you doing here?"

"Well, I followed you," Cally admitted. "From school."

"You followed me? From school?"

"So no damage done to the hearing, then. And yeah. I thought, well, I thought you might need someone to talk to."

"*You* did?" Ben was having trouble with the concept. "Nobody else bothered apart from you, Cally? And after the way I treated you last year over the Stromfeld program?" The guilt just kept on coming.

"Last year is old news, Ben," said Cally.

"But I tried to force you out. Why should you worry what happens to me?"

"Because you went to the Centennial Club." Cally counted on her fingers. "Because you're a good secret agent. Because you can't let this business with Lori and Jake poison your whole life. Because the team needs you, leader or not. Because you've got nice buns, though that's more of a bonus. . . ."

"You've run out of fingers," Ben observed.

"No problem. I've run out of points, too."

"Well, I think you've probably made your main one." Ben sighed. "I don't know what I was doing coming here. Running away doesn't help anyone. Okay, Cal," he resolved, "you can call it mission accomplished. Ben Stanton is on his way back."

The face of the psimurai, shrunken and withered, was displayed on the screen of the smart-desk in Briefing Room One. Bond Team, Corporal Keene, and Senior Tutor Elmore Grant regarded it with a mixture of curiosity and distaste.

"Maybe he just worked out," suggested Eddie.

"The techs have performed a complete physical analysis on the subject," Grant said. "His muscles are so atrophied that he could barely have stood up in the armor, let alone engaged in vigorous acts of violence. But there's more. We ran DNA and retina checks —"

"But if he's not on a criminal database —"

"He doesn't have to be, Jake," Grant responded, raising an eyebrow at the interruption. *Hah!* Ben nearly burst out. *That's one in the eye for you, Daly.* "We have access to other kinds of records. Many corporations, particularly those whose business interests are in the more sensitive areas of the economy, now insist on storing the DNA codes of their employees for security purposes. Retina scans are taken of all entrants into the country, however long they intend to stay. The long and short of it all is that the techs did indeed come up with a match for our wizened warrior." Grant paused.

"Give us a clue," said Eddie. "How many syllables?"

"The man's name is Hiro Nagashima."

Bex and Ben exchanged stupefied glances.

"But that's just not possible, sir," complained Bex. "I know there's probably more than one guy in the world called Nagashima — only it can't be a coincidence — and maybe the light wasn't too good in the Centennial Club, probably so nobody had to see the old codgers spilling their drinks —"

"But this Nagashima can't be our Nagashima," Ben concluded. "Bex is right."

"Hiro Nagashima," Grant read from a sheet of paper in front of him. "Japanese national. Born 1982. Founder and chairman of Nagashima Industries. Specializing in nuclear technology and new kinds of energy. It was a Nagashima plant that was sabotaged during the Great Contamination of the 2020s. No immediate family. Immensely wealthy. Increasingly reclusive. Not many photographs or film records of Nagashima in the public realm, but have a look at this one, taken at the time of the disaster at his plant, so some forty years ago. Desk: Show photo."

The smart-desk obeyed. Ben and Bex both gaped.

"That's him!" Bex tapped her finger on the Japanese man's

forehead for emphasis. "That's Nagashima. That's the guy we saw at the club."

"You'd have had to have gone through a time warp to see *him* at the club, Bex," Eddie said. "Forty years adds a few wrinkles."

Ben sat back thoughtfully. An impossibly young Nagashima holding forth to a ring of old men as creakingly ancient as the psimurai, who was apparently also Nagashima. "A specialist in new kinds of energy. Life is what we are offering," Ben recalled him saying. The secret of successful espionage was to bring together disparate strands of information and to combine them in a way that made sense, like artists mixing single colors to create a multihued masterpiece. Ben was mixing his colors quietly. He wasn't quite ready to show off his painting.

Grant was drawing the meeting to a close, in any case. Bond Team had something else important to do. Ben detected a sympathetic glance from Cally, a vaguely embarrassed one from Lori, and studious avoidance of his sight line by Jake.

It was time to elect a new leader.

The votes were in. With an electorate of six, they didn't take long to count.

The winner received the congratulations from the rest of Bond Team with all due humility and tried to ignore the fact that Ben was in the room for the announcement. Then, as soon as it was polite, Ben was to leave the others behind and find some space to be alone, to think. The Hall of Heroes fitted the bill.

Bond Team already had a presence here, and its members hadn't even graduated yet. Among the Fallen, those students of Spy High who had made the ultimate sacrifice in the cause, was a holographic Jennifer Chen, hovering as if she were immortal, a sleeping goddess who might at any moment open her eyes, stretch, yawn, and step down from her plinth to rejoin the living. As if. Bond Team's only casualty so far, but the future could bring others. And leadership certainly brought with it responsibility. Decisions might have to be made, which could endanger a teammate's life even to the point of providing poor Jennifer with a companion. Did Bond Team's new leader have the courage to take that responsibility? And the will to make those decisions?

At the hall's far end, where the victors in the Sherlock Shield competition were triumphantly displayed, Bond Team appeared again — last year's champions. Did its new leader have the strength not to let success go to her head, not to allow power or glory to become its own end, its own reward?

The others evidently thought so. She had cast her vote for Jake, but her teammates had unanimously selected her to replace Ben — even Ben himself. That had to mean something.

Faith in herself. It had always been an Achilles heel. The blonde hair and blue eyes, the cheerleader's figure — so many people had never really looked beyond the surface that sometimes Lori had also been tempted to believe that she had nothing else to offer.

Sometimes. And almost.

Grant had believed in her. Spy High had saved her from a life of simpering predictability. And now her teammates, too, had resoundingly expressed their confidence in her abilities. Effectively, they'd entrusted her with their lives. So whatever doubts she might have she needed to dismiss. She couldn't let the others down. She couldn't let herself down. It was time to prove herself once and for all.

With determination like blue steel in her eyes, Lori Angel strode purposefully from the Hall of Heroes.

Of course he wasn't in the Photo-Editing Suite to hide from the others. Not Ben Stanton. So what if Lori was team leader now instead of him? He'd voted for her himself — at least nobody would be able to accuse him of sour grapes. Good luck to her. She'd probably need it. Taking charge of a Spy High team wasn't quite as easy as he'd made it look, a fact Lori would no doubt learn in due course.

No, Ben was actually busy, engrossed in picture research. He had a few ideas about Hiro Nagashima that he wanted to explore, and he was starting by raiding Deveraux Academy's photographic data banks. Millions of still images were stored here, everything from the earliest sepia photographs to the three-dimensional color spreads culled from this morning's newspapers. Visual records of Hiro Nagashima came somewhere between the two, and as Grant had forewarned, they were not numerous.

Ben had sorted them in chronological order. Nagashima as little more than a teenager, a genius in his field even then, a pioneer of new ideas for energy at the dawn of a new century. Older, in his prime, at the time of the nuclear plant disaster, the man Ben had seen, however impossibly, at the Centennial Club. Then older still, more like the man in the psimurai armor, entering a hoverlimo and reluctant to be photographed, bodyguards bulging into the shot. That was the last entry Ben had found, taken some five years ago. There was something about it that bothered him.

Ben leaned back in his chair thoughtfully. It was getting to be a habit. *Okay, so you didn't want yourself plastered over the papers for whatever reason. Fair enough. And you've got bodyguards the size of the Rockies to dissuade photographers from taking liberties. Fair enough again. But if you really wanted your face kept safe from prying lenses, why not also cover it with your hands or your arm or pull your jacket up over your head, like guys being taken into police custody?* Nagashima wasn't doing any of that. In fact, his hands were in front of him, apparently attempting to block the camera's view of the interior of the hover-limo, like there was something inside he particularly didn't want to be so much as glimpsed.

Or someone.

And wasn't that the faintest outline of a man Ben could make out between Nagashima's gnarled fingers? Maybe he should look more closely. He used the Photo Editor's facility to divide the image into a grid and selected the appropriate section for enlargement. He was left with very big fingers and definitely a man in the limo waiting for Nagashima. He drew up a new grid, enlarged again. Now Ben could distinguish the lower half of a face in profile, the chin, the ear and hair, most of the nose. Still very dark, though. Ben had the image cleaned, lightened. It was a black man in the car. And now, the final technique. Just as forensic scientists had been doing for years, the Photo Editor could employ its preprogrammed knowledge of anatomy to reconstruct an entire human body from a given detail. In this case, Ben judged, just the head would do.

He couldn't believe the result.

"Ben? Can I come in?" Rather strangely, Cally was at the door.

"Afraid there's no lunatic with a psionic sword for you to save me from at the moment, Cal," Ben said, "though if you hang around for a bit, you never know your luck."

"I just wondered if you were all right." Pause. "You know, after the election."

"Did you?" Ben didn't quite know how to take Cally's concern. "Well, uh, thanks. I guess."

"I mean, is there anything I can . . ."

Ben grinned, like the old Ben, the Ben who'd been team leader. "Yeah. There is, Cal, actually. Get the others. I've got something to show you all."

"Nagashima getting into a limo," Bex said with Bond Team gathered in the Photo-Editing Suite. "Nice. Do we assume this means something?"

"Ben must have his reasons," Lori admonished.

"Oh, I do," Ben assured them, interested by Lori's support. "This picture was taken in 2057 when Nagashima was defending his company against a lawsuit brought by the descendents of victims of the nuclear plant sabotage back in the Great Contamination. Seems there's been almost constant litigation against Nagashima Industries since then, down the generations. Seems some people think all that nuclear waste escaping across the Southwest wasn't the consequence of a terrorist outrage, after all, which is the official line, but a deliberate act on the part of Nagashima Industries and with its namesake and chairman's absolute knowledge and consent."

"But why, Ben?" Cally wanted to know. "What would be the gain? It was that leak that created the Wasteland, hundreds of square miles rendered completely desolate, unfit for any kind of life."

Ben shrugged. "Good question. Maybe the idea was to

discredit nuclear energy and increase investment in the alternative energy programs that Nagashima was already working on. I don't know. But it's worth noting that the Temple of the Transformation's head office, Temple Prime as we know it's called, is located right there in the middle of the Wasteland. Thanks to some pretty radical environmending, needless to say."

"I'm pleased for the Wasteland," Eddie said. "But aren't we getting away from the photo?"

"I don't think so," said Ben. "Look. Even at this magnification, you can just about see a passenger already in the limo." Ben outlined what he'd done with the image. "And guess who this guy turned out to be."

"Dr. Frankenstein?" groaned Eddie. "He usually turns up every five minutes."

"Not this time he doesn't." Ben pressed a button.

"Gabriel," gasped Cally. "It's Gabriel."

The founder and spiritual leader of the Temple of the Transformation stared out at Bond Team from the Photo Editor. His eyes were white and blind — the anatomy program lacked the imagination to pick a color — but every other detail registered with Cally instantly.

"So there is a connection between Nagashima and the Temple, between the Temple and the Centennial Club, between both and Mac's death." Cally looked like she might be about to throw her arms around Ben's neck. "I *knew* the Temple had to figure somewhere. Ben, you don't know what this means to me."

"Well, can you wait to tell him until the rest of us have maybe left the room?" said Bex squeamishly. "I think this might be best kept between the two of you."

"Good work, Ben," Jake conceded, nodding unenvious approval.

"Yeah, good," echoed Eddie, "and good for Cally, too, but could someone please explain what the heck this Gabriel guy's supposed to mean to *me*?"

"Ben and Bex said that at the club, Nagashima referred to the Temple Prime operation," Lori reminded Eddie. "And now it's clear that he also knows, or knew, Gabriel, too." She was suddenly aware that her teammates were regarding her expectantly. She realized why. First big leadership decision coming up. "I think it's time we paid a visit to Temple Prime ourselves."

PART
TWO

It was the short straw, Cally knew, a straw nearly as short as the skirt she'd reluctantly wriggled into, but there was no alternative. The Bond Teamer to visit the Temple's church had to be her. She was the only one who'd met Timothy before, and he was the only one who could help them.

A female disciple with the body language of a rabbit in fear of its life directed her to Timothy's office, one of those private rooms he'd talked about. Obviously the Temple didn't have any hang-ups about modern technology: Timothy was hard at work on a computer. When he saw who his visitor was, however, what he was doing suddenly didn't seem quite as important.

"Cally!" Immediate surprise swiftly mastered by the official voice of the disciple. "May Gabriel be praised, you have returned to us." A sideways snap at the rabbit: "That'll be all, Bathsheba." As the girl departed, Timothy approached Cally. "I've prayed that you might come back, that you might see the light and save your soul."

Yeah, right, Cally scoffed inwardly. *Well, if you're so interested in my soul, how come your eyes are glued to my legs?* But, "I know," she said shyly. "I haven't been able to forget the Temple's message since the gathering. I haven't been able to forget *you,* Timothy."

"Really?" the disciple gulped." I mean, it's never too late to give yourself to the Temple, Cally, or to seek . . . comfort from its loyal servants."

His ogling had graduated to her bare midriff now. Sadly,

Bex had been right. Dress to kill and Timothy'd be putty in her hands. If only she hadn't been talked into displaying *quite* so much naked skin. Sometimes she wore more than this in the shower. The things she did for Spy High. . . .

"I think," Cally fluttered, "I'm in need of a little bit of Transformation, Timothy."

"Then you've come to the right place." Was he trying to look seductive or was that just a nervous twitch? He gestured to a leather sofa along the wall. "Shall we be seated?"

"Soon," she promised, "but first, Timothy, there's a teensy-weensy little favor I'd like to ask." She brought her thumbs and forefingers close together to show exactly how teensy-weensy it was.

"Ask and it will be given," said Timothy generously.

"Well, when we spoke last time, you said you could send disciples to Temple Prime, to be close to Gabriel himself."

"Of course. All I need to do is enter a disciple's details into the computer here and then that blessed individual can travel to live and work at the very heart of the Temple."

"You see," Cally pursued, "that's what I think I'd like most of all, to be at the heart of the Temple."

"Ah," continued Timothy, "but only the most special of disciples are chosen to go to Temple Prime, only those with the greatest potential for . . . study and worship."

Cally wiggled her hips a little, lazily flicked her dreadlocks. "And do you think I might have potential, Timothy?"

"Perhaps we'd better find out." He indicated the sofa again. "Shall we?"

"If you think it'll help," Cally said. "Just one second, though." She opened her handbag, reached inside, and drew out a small bottle of what looked like perfume. Looked like, but wasn't. "Just need to freshen up a little," she winked.

And sprayed the scent in his face.

Timothy's eyes widened. He thought about flinching back and protesting, but didn't manage either. He wouldn't manage anything for a good fifteen minutes. Cally had temporarily paralyzed him with a stasis spray, giving her plenty of time not only to enter Bond Team's names into the computer without him ever knowing but also to take her leave and never have to see disciple Timothy again.

Cally patted him on the cheek. "Praise be to Gabriel," she said.

Jonathan Deveraux resided on the top floor of the school that bore his name. His accommodations consisted of one huge metallic room of sensors and circuitry, a computerized cocoon that he never left. There were no easy chairs because he never needed to sit. There was no bed because he never needed to sleep. And "resided" was the right word. It was debatable whether Jonathan Deveraux could be said to *live* anywhere at all. Not when the human form of the man had ceased to exist ten years previously.

Jonathan Deveraux was, effectively, software.

But Bex still liked to come and see him. He was her father, after all. He could talk to her via a digitalized reconstruction of his original voice and look at her from the giant screens that circled the room: one face or a hundred faces, all perfect. What he couldn't do, of course, was hold her. But what teenage girl with piercings and purple hair would ever want to be held by her father, anyway?

"I just wanted to say good-bye." Bex was alone with him now. "Before we hit the Temple trail, if you know what I mean. And I wanted to thank you, Dad."

"Thank me?" As if the concept of gratitude was an alien one.

"Sure. For agreeing to us going on this mission. We were worried after we'd done all the groundwork you might still let a graduate team pull rank on us."

A single Jonathan Deveraux split into two and each gave a reason. "You are younger than a graduate team, less likely to be suspected of ulterior motives in penetrating the Temple. You have firsthand knowledge that may prove vital during operations." The faces blended back together. "Bond Team has been assigned. The members of Bond Team have been granted exceptional leave from their studies for the maximum period of a week."

"Yeah, can't stay away for long, can we?" Bex said.

"Exams coming up soon." Her father seemed to have no comment on this matter. "So it wasn't favoritism why we were chosen then?"

"Favoritism?" Another idea that seemed to have been omitted from Jonathan Deveraux's data banks.

"Because I'm your daughter, yeah." And perhaps Bex was beginning to wish she'd left on the mission without a final word with her father. If he pondered, "daughter?", in that same tone of voice, like a bad tape recording . . .

"No, Rebecca," said Jonathan Deveraux, as cold as the screen that bore his image. "Your assignment was not due to favoritism because you are my daughter."

But somehow, Bex found herself wishing it had been.

* * *

Ben caught up with Lori in the rec room. It was difficult to tell whether she was pleased to be alone with him or not.

"I haven't got long, Ben." Her barriers were already going up. "A last quick cup of Spy High coffee before we leave. Who knows what they'll serve us at Temple Prime?"

"Yeah, well, this won't take long. You can spare a few minutes for an ex-boyfriend fallen on hard times, can't you, Lo?"

"Ben, don't."

"It's all right. I won't. I didn't come here to give you a hard time."

Lori studied him. He was still good-looking, still very blond and very square-jawed, but there was no going back. "It was good of you to volunteer to be our home contact, Ben, I meant to say earlier. We'll need someone reliable in case anything goes wrong on the mission. But I can guess how difficult it'll likely be for you, staying in school while the rest of us are out in the field."

"I can live with it," Ben shrugged, though Lori was, of course, correct. "I want to keep researching Nagashima, see what I can find. Besides, Lori, I don't think it'd be the best idea for you on your first operation as team leader to have a previous leader kind of lurking in the background. This'll give you a chance to establish your own authority."

"Thanks, Ben. That's thoughtful." *Unusually so*, Lori pondered.

"'Cause let me tell you, Lo, this is what I wanted to tell you, leadership is tough. You need to keep on your toes."

"I did ballet for eight years, Ben," smiled Lori. "I know about keeping on my toes."

"Yeah, well . . ."

"No, I'm sorry." If she squeezed his hand, would it be misconstrued? (A leader had to make decisions.) "Thanks." She

squeezed his hand. "I appreciate the advice. You set a fine example for Bond Team, Ben. I just hope I can live up to it."

Ben nodded. "Well, I think there's an outside chance." Lori
laughed. "Oh, and Lo, one last thing."

"What is it?"

"The new hairstyle. It's good."

"You know in cartoons? The really old ones? You know when
Scooby-Doo and Shaggy are being chased by a janitor in a
sheet and the background keeps repeating itself every five seconds—the same painting on the wall, the same chest of draw-
ers? You know what I'm talking about?" It was probable that his
teammates did know what Eddie was talking about. They just
weren't listening. "Well, that's what I think we've got happening
here." He gazed out of the hoverbus window mournfully. "We're
not heading for Temple Prime at all. We're in a cartoon." The
desert surrounded them in all directions, stony, featureless,
bleached clean of life, seemingly stretching to the ends of the
earth. "And what's worse, it isn't even *funny*."

Lori's attention was focused more on the inside of the bus,
on their fellow recruits. Most of them were young, some even
younger than Bond Team, and all wore the fixed and excited
smiles of children about to arrive at the Magic Kingdom for the
first time. Lori nudged a sullen Jake alongside her, who obviously disapproved of the expressions on their co-passengers'
faces "Cheer up," she said "Those are the smiles we've got to
match."

"Yeah?" Jake grumbled. "Those are the smiles normally produced by lobotomies."

"They're happy to be going to Temple Prime, Jake. They're

going to live in the Temple, be with the blessed Gabriel himself. This is their dream coming true. We've got to look just like them, or we're going to be found out before we even get started."

"I know." Jake scowled. "But if you ask me, their dream's more like a nightmare."

"Hey," Cally signaled from the seat in front. "Up ahead."

The whole bus seemed to stir. There was some spontaneous applause, cries of jubilation that spread down the aisle like a particularly virulent virus. A girl across the way from Bex clasped her hands above her heart and closed her eyes and fervently prayed: "Hallelujah. Hallelujah. Hallelujah."

Temple Prime lay ahead.

There was the blue of a lake and the ribboned azure of rivers and the lush green of fields bearing crops that ought not to grow in the heart of this sterile wilderness. There were clusters of long, simple wooden buildings, single-story and little more than huts. But Cally frowned in puzzlement. Where was the pyramid? On the footage Mac had downloaded, there'd been a pyramid. Now there wasn't.

"Not exactly Las Vegas, is it?" Eddie grunted.

And Bex had spotted something else. A fence, tall and made of wire, conceivably electrified but certainly extending around the entire perimeter of Temple Prime. *To keep unbelievers out?* she wondered. *Or believers in?*

"The . . . Host!" someone joyed. "The Host has come to greet us!"

Jake peered out of the window, directly into the sun. He was temporarily dazzled, blinded, but as his sight returned it seemed to him that there were angels in the sky, figures robed in white. It seemed, briefly, that they had wings. Even more briefly,

Jake wondered whether he was hallucinating. But as his vision became clearer, so did the truth. Not angels. Guys with jet packs that *looked* like wings. The members of the Heavenly Host were the teachers of the Temple, the ordinary disciples' superiors and ordained to wear white, to signify the Transformation from sin to purity, Jake had learned. He regarded the bogus angels grimly as they accompanied the bus through the gates of Temple Prime. He wasn't fooled. They were the Temple's shock troops, the kind of guys who always got in your way on missions. They'd need watching.

Not that there seemed anything hostile or dangerous about the Host as it lined up to welcome the recruits to their new home. Rather the opposite, in fact. The men and women in white were charming, delighted to meet the arrivals, certain that their lives would now be changed forever, provided with fresh purpose and direction. It was curious, Lori thought. Grant and Jonathan Deveraux had given them pretty much the same kind of speech when they joined Spy High.

One of the hosts called Peter, his dark hair long and flowing, was directing the recruits to follow him, like a kind of angelic tour guide. Apparently, the blessed Gabriel wished to speak to the latest of his children.

"Gabriel . . . ," the word went around. "Gabriel himself . . . We're really going to see him . . ."

"Isn't this wonderful?" a young man with shining eyes addressed Eddie.

"Yes. Yes, it is." Eddie didn't want to disappoint him.

"Isn't this just the best moment of your life?"

"Well, you know . . . it's up there."

"Would you like to link hands with me so our souls can be one?"

"Actually, I just need to speak to my friend over there. . . ."

Peter led them through the site. It seemed clear to Lori that the wooden huts were the disciples' accommodation blocks, communal dormitories. Most of the actual disciples were at work in the fields, but some they passed by. Lori was horrified. Their faces were empty of emotion. Their movements sluggish and slow, like sleepwalkers. *How long did it take for Temple Prime to sap your spirit to this extent? A week? A month?* The new arrivals, so eager, so desperate to find a meaning in their lives, they didn't know what they were letting themselves in for. Inspiration? More like indoctrination.

The group reached an enormous area of bare, flat land. Its immediate purpose seemed mysterious, but at the heart of Temple Prime, it had to have some significance. Peter was halting them before it.

"The pyramid," Cally hissed in her ear.

And then Peter's arms were thrown wide in supplication. "Once," he boomed, "this was barren earth, a wasteland created by the wickedness of man."

"Nagashima Industries and a few alleged terrorists, to be precise," whispered Eddie.

"Shush, Eddie," Bex scolded, "or we won't hear him."

In actual fact, there wasn't likely to be any problem with hearing Peter. Either he'd suddenly been able to gain several hundred decibels in volume merely from diaphragm exercises, or else his voice was now being amplified by any number of hidden loudspeakers around Temple Prime.

"But Gabriel came here. The herald of the Lord led him here, and to Gabriel the herald said, "'This is the place.'"

Cally knew the words. She'd read the file. "In this place build a Temple to the Lord, the likes of which will never have been seen before.'"

The ground beneath their feet began to tremble, as if waking from a restless sleep. It began to shake. Many of the recruits cried out. Bond Team did not.

"'From the very ashes of destruction,'" Peter powered, "'will rise the Temple of the Transformation. . . .'"

And now the ground before them was splitting open, like a fatal wound in the flesh of the soil, and beneath was darkness lit by impossible light. Several recruits were dropping to their knees in awe, hands raised high. "It's showtime, folks," Jake murmured.

"'. . . and its light will cover all the world.'"

The pyramid thrust upward, the glittering golden cross at its apex first, then the highest levels of its four sides, not sheer, not smooth, but each indented from its neighbor below like a series of steps in concrete and steel. The upper levels seemed to be constructed entirely of glass banded by metal. Each tier was the height of a man.

"That's what I call technology," observed Eddie.

"There's big money behind the Temple," Cally agreed. "Whatever they say in their fake bible, Gabriel didn't call on the power of God to create Temple Prime in the middle of the desert. He called on the latest environmending techniques, and they cost huge."

"Maybe his old mate Nagashima lended a hand," commented Jake.

And still the pyramid rose, tall and towering, gigantic now, dwarfing the disciples. The space that had been flat and empty before them was now filled with the crowning glory of the Temple of the Transformation. There was the hiss of hidden gears and unseen mechanisms as the pyramid's base locked into position. A ramp extended from what seemed like the main entrance several levels above the ground.

"Fancy a look around, leader lady?" Jake hinted.

"I think a little tour might be in order, "acknowledged Lori.

"Look! Look!" The shining eyes of the young man who'd spoken to Eddie were also sharp. "Up at the cross! It's Gabriel!"

A sigh of adulation shuddered through the assembled recruits. Bond Team did their best to echo it, though Cally in particular looked more as if she was about to be violently sick.

Gabriel stood on a platform by the cross, gazing down with wise benevolence on those who had abandoned their lives to join him. He nodded in approval at their choice.

"He's gonna give a speech now, isn't he?" Eddie groaned. "Full of the joys of Transformation and all that stuff, isn't he? Do you think they'd notice if we just . . ." He made walking motions with his fingers.

"Stay where you are, Eddie," warned Lori. "You're in the Temple now."

Didn't he know it. After enduring Gabriel's speech for almost an hour — "and if I had a credit for every time the Big Man mentioned Transformation . . ." — there was still no respite. Then the sexes were separated and accompanied by a member of the Host into long chambers in the base of the pyramid, chambers where walls, floors, and ceilings flickered with lights.

Peter had remained with the males. "The lowest level of the pyramid," he explained. "Still within the blessed Gabriel's sight but also far from the rapture of final Transformation." ("If I had a dollar . . . ," Eddie began.) "But here you begin your rebirth as disciples of the one true faith. Here you begin your ascent toward . . ."

"Don't tell me," muttered Eddie.

Apparently, rebirth also began with stripping off their clothes.

"What? With everyone looking?" Eddie was shocked. "What about my modesty?" He grudgingly hauled off his shirt. "They could at least have left boys and girls together for this bit. Might have made it worth coming."

"You discard your clothes as you discard all trappings of your lives," Peter was pointing out. "And as you garb yourselves in the simple black of the disciples of the Temple, you demonstrate to yourselves and to the world your commitment to the cause of Transformation, your undying pledge to devote yourselves to study and prayer. Indeed, in time some of you here may even prove yourselves worthy to be raised to the rank of the Host, purifying through piety your black into white."

"Yeah, yeah," muttered a naked Eddie. "Right now I'm worried about turning blue. Can we get the new kit *on*, please?"

"Dress," allowed Peter, "and make yourselves new."

There were black robes for everyone, loose-fitting and hooded — "to cover our heads in humility," Jake heard somebody say — and with matching black slippers for the feet. "Actually," Eddie said, "They're not too bad. You could start a line of designer cult wear with these. You know — what the fashionable religious fanatic is wearing this season."

"If only the Temple insisted on a vow of silence," Jake grumbled.

"Now come," Peter was beckoning. "Before you are reunited

with your fellow disciples, there is one final duty for me to perform. Your names, too, are part of the lives you have left behind. They must also change."

"Dare I hope for Brad?" said Eddie.

"Enoch?" Bex could barely stifle a giggle. "That's real catchy, Ed."

"Typical, isn't it? The old Nelligan luck, all bad." The five members of Bond Team were at a trestle table partaking of their first evening meal at Temple Prime. "And then Jakey goes and gets Luke. Strong, proud, single syllable. I mean, is that a first-prize name or what?"

"I don't care what he's called," said Lori, smiling at Jake.

"Oh, please, Lori," Bex winced. "Not while we're eating."

"So what about you girls, anyway?" Jake said. "What are we going to have to call you now?"

"Oh, us," Cally grinned. "Meet Martha," (pointing to herself) "Mary," (to Lori) "and Delilah."

"Delilah?" Now it was Eddie's turn to regard Bex with amusement. "If only I'd got Samson we might have had a good time. But Bex — why the hooded look?" Bex's hood was indeed covering her head while her companions' were down. "You suddenly scared to show us your face?"

"Not while you're around, Enoch," Bex said, "but why I think they called me Delilah has something to do with hair. Sadly, purple doesn't fit into the Temple's color scheme." She drew back her hood.

Bex's head had been shaved.

Whatever he did, however hard he tried, he couldn't put the others out of his mind.

Work had been his first attempt, more practice, struggling to occupy himself so completely with the theoretical that the practical dangers possibly facing his teammates at this very moment might slip his memory. It hadn't happened.

So he'd turned his restless attention back to Hiro Nagashima, trawling through the IGC data banks a second and a third time in case there was something he'd missed. There wasn't. And Ben wasn't Cally. So far his hacking skills had not been sufficient to crack Nagashima Industries' computer codes. And when he found himself (rather unexpectedly) wishing that Cally was still at Spy High, he necessarily remembered why she wasn't, and why he was. It didn't improve his mood.

He resorted to the final refuge of someone wanting to forget his problems: a game of pool in the recreation room. And even here there was trouble, summed up in two words: Simon Macey.

"What's this, Stanton?" Macey and a couple of his usual chorus of grinning idiots sauntered over when they saw Ben at the table. "Playing on your own tonight?"

"Why, Simon? Want a game?" Ben continued potting balls without looking up. As much as he might want to, it would not be wise for him to rise to Macey's taunts at the moment. Self-control and self-discipline. That was the way back.

"None of your teammates wanted to take you on? Oh, no, of course." Simon Macey tutted, clicked his fingers. "They can't, can they? They're all out on operational duty and you've been relegated to home contact, haven't you? Funny how most missions don't bother with home contacts, though, isn't it, Stanton? First they take the leadership away from you and now this. Do you think they're trying to tell you something?"

"Why, Simon? Are you?" A center pocket shot. The cue ball rolled down to the far end of the table.

"I hear the luscious Lori told you something." Macey grinned to his companions. "Please accept my heartfelt sympathies at the breakdown of your relationship, but I'm sure it didn't come as a surprise."

About the same as what's coming next, Ben wagered silently. At the opposite end of the table to Simon Macey, he lined up the shot.

"She was always far too good for you, Stanton. Everybody knew it."

Self-control and self-discipline, yes. But a little bit of payback, too.

"And I'm sure the rest of us are only too pleased the angelic one is available again."

"Why, Simon? Think you've got a chance? I don't think so." Ben struck the cue ball. Low. Hard. It shot off the table like a miniature cannonball, hit Simon Macey precisely where a member of the male sex least wants to be hit. Maybe Macey was still leering while he was doubled up in pain, but Ben doubted it. "I don't know," he sighed. "I just can't seem to get that shot right. Anyone else want a go?"

And normally, any triumph over Simon Macey, however petty, would leave Ben in laughter. But not tonight.

Whatever he did, however hard he tried, he couldn't put the others out of his mind.

Much later, and with the disciples in the dormitories sleeping with the soundness of clear consciences, it was simple for Bond Team to creep outside and to congregate conspiratorially at the prearranged spot.

"Okay, let's keep this short and sweet," Lori whispered. "There may not be much security in the dorms, but I don't want to have to explain why we're out of bed to a Host patrol. Anyone found out anything useful?"

"Just think of the money Bex is going to save on shampoo and hair dye."

"Eddie, *useful*."

"Well, there's nothing we can learn out here." Cally cast a contemptuous eye over the dormitories and the dark field beyond. "If the Temple's got secrets, they're kept in the pyramid."

More impressive than ever by night, its outline lit like a silhouette of fire.

"And we're not going to get in there too easily, either," contributed Jake soberly. "Eddie and I tried it earlier. Thought if anyone stopped us or anything on our first day, we could plead ignorance. We got to the top of the ramp all right but then . . ."

"The Host came down upon us," Eddie added, "and there was *much* pleading of ignorance."

"At least you'd have been convincing, Enoch," said Bex. She turned to Lori. "I've been talking with Ruth, she's one of the women in white, and *she* told me the pyramid symbolizes the assent toward Transformation. Everybody starts off at the bottom, but only a few ever manage to make the top. The higher tiers, those reached by ramp and above, are accessible only to the Host. We mere disciples aren't worthy enough yet. We have to wait until we earn our white robes."

"Gonna be a long wait," muttered Jake.

"Something else she said was interesting, though," Bex pursued. "Apparently, every now and again some lucky disciple who's shown the greatest commitment to the cause is chosen to be a missionary. You know, to go out and spread the word of Gabriel to the unbelieving multitudes. Ruth said they *do* get taken right to the top of the pyramid, to meet with Gabriel and receive his blessing and all that kind of stuff before they leave Temple Prime for good. Seems they go in, and that's the last the other disciples see of them. She said she hoped *I* might get chosen one day. I didn't really like the sound of it. Anyway, the highest level of all is supposedly where the Temple of Tranquillity is. It's the point of Transformation itself."

"Then that's where we've got to go," decided Lori.

"How are we going to do that?" Eddie asked. "I don't fancy hanging around here long enough to join the Host or become a missionary just so we can get inside a pyramid."

"All right," said Lori. "We don't go *inside* the pyramid at all."

"Say again?"

Lori thumbed at the structure's stepped and slanted sides. "We take the scenic route."

CHAPTER ELEVEN

"Well, I guess we ought to look on the positive side," said Eddie. "It's a great view from up here, isn't it? Much higher and we might be able to see all the way back to Deveraux."

"Eddie," Lori disapproved, "this isn't a class field trip. Thanks for the commentary, but can we have a little more focus on the climbing?"

Eddie grunted. "And I thought Ben was a hard taskmaster."

He didn't like to admit it to the others, but he hadn't paused solely to make smart comments (that was just a bonus). He'd stopped because he needed a few seconds to catch his breath and rest. Scaling the pyramid was not easy.

Bond Team was more than halfway to the top of the massive structure, but there still seemed a painfully long way to go. Eddie's limbs were beginning to feel like plasticine, and it was just as well it was night. Not only did the darkness, combined with the black of their robes, help obscure their progress from possible prying eyes — Host patrols and the like — but it also prevented his teammates from noticing that his complexion was now as red as his hair. And he'd thought he was fit. Maybe he'd have been coping more manfully if they hadn't also spent the whole day laboring in the fields along with their fellow disciples, sweating hard, and singing hymns to the glory of Gabriel. He hadn't seen very much to sing about himself. Cally had whispered in his ear that this must have been what slavery was like in the old days.

"I don't know, Lori." Bex was propped up against the side of the pyramid and panting. "I'm with Eddie. Can't hurt to take five, can it? We've come a long way."

"Could have done with five pairs of Host wings," said Cally.

"Bex," said Lori, perhaps regretfully but still with finality, "we can't even afford to take *one*. If we get seen up here, our cover's blown. There'll be time to chill when we've done what we set out to do, not before."

"But Lori . . . ," began Bex.

"No 'buts' on missions," Jake suddenly snapped. "'But' isn't a word you use to your team leader, Bex. Lori's right. Let's go."

"Yeah, yeah. Sorry."

Bex bent low and made a stirrup with her hands for Eddie to step on. Up he scrambled onto the next tier of the pyramid before leaning back over the edge and helping to heave Bex after him. Jake was carrying out the same procedure. Cally was keeping watch until her teammates had completed the operation, and then was pulled up by them in her turn. *Then* they repeated the whole process. The triangle above them was starting to shrink.

"What you said to Bex, Jake," Lori whispered to her boyfriend as he helped her higher, "I appreciate the support, but there wasn't any need. I would have dealt with it."

"I know," Jake said.

"I've got to learn how to cope with situations in the field as team leader."

"I know." Jake sneaked a quick kiss on her cheek. "You're doing fine."

"You didn't use to do that to Ben when he was doing fine as well, did you?" Lori regarded Jake with mock suspicion.

"After all this time," Jake grinned, "my secret is out."

The cross was coming closer.

It hadn't escaped Eddie's attention that, of all five of them, only Bex was wearing her hood up. Maybe the enforced bald look was making her sensitive. The thought made Eddie feel strange, kind of protective somehow, kind of serious. Not his usual self at all.

"It'll grow back, you know," he told her. "Your hair, I mean."

"Thanks, Ed," Bex said with exaggerated gratitude, "but even if it doesn't, it'll be easier managing with no hair than no brains."

"Guys, look." Cally was pointing toward the summit of the pyramid, now very near indeed. They were just a few levels from the great glass slabs that housed the Temple of Tranquillity.

"Just what we need." Eddie reverted to type. "A place to take a break."

The conclusion of their climb in sight, the Bond Teamers found the strength to reach the glass peak quickly. They had to move more carefully now, though. Light was emanating from this part of the pyramid. Something was going on within, something that maybe only dared take place at night.

The five students pressed their faces against the glass and peered inside.

At least Ben's little altercation with Macey had produced one positive benefit. Two, if you counted seeing the leader of Solo Team reduced to shuffling along the corridor half bent over like an old man. It had refueled his determination to do *something* to help his teammates in the field, however limited that aid might be. It had taken him back to the computer.

He could access the public face of Hiro Nagashima, no problem. It was delving beneath that was difficult. Cally's hacking was intuitive, which was why she was so good at it. She could make a system love her, be eager to reveal its secrets for her. Ben had enough trouble making people even *like* him, and he was no more natural with technology. But he did have a forceful personality, that could not be denied, and he was a Stanton — he never gave up — and for the sake of the others and for the sake of his own self-esteem, he *would* never give up. He'd crack Nagashima's security codes. Ben Stanton always got what he wanted in the end.

This time, in the end, took a little under four hours.

But time didn't matter. He had time. And now he was in. A long list of Nagashima's personal files was displayed before him. They were in Japanese, of course, but the Spy High's system's Babel chip translated them instantly. Ben scrolled down. Which would be useful and which would not?

SPECIAL PROJECTS. Ben clicked on it. It should have said "Jackpot."

Two special projects only — Nagashima obviously didn't like to spread his genius too thinly — and of one of them Ben already had firsthand experience. It probably wasn't necessary for him to click on PSIMURAI.

SOUL STEALER, however, that was a different matter.

Ben clicked, frowned. To fully access Soul Stealer he needed to enter a supplementary password. He thought of Nagashima and Gabriel, old men and young disciples, the Centennial Club and Temple Prime. . . . There was only one word that Ben could type in here. He did so.

TRANSFORMATION.

The Soul Stealer file opened in obedience for Ben's inspection. "Good day, Mr. Nagashima," the computer said with politeness.

What Ben said was not polite, and untranslatable even by the Babel chip.

"Doesn't look much like a temple to me," observed Eddie. "What happened to the altars and the incense burners? I thought they were in every temple's contract."

"Somehow, Ed," mused Cally darkly, "I don't think prayer's on the menu."

The Temple of Tranquillity, if that was indeed what Bond Team was gazing down upon — the walls of the pyramid functioning as a slanted ceiling for a floor tens of meters below — did indeed resemble a lab for scientific research rather than a place of worship. Dynamos throbbed, brimming with power they could hardly contain. And around the dynamos, four in number, were consoles and computers, monitoring instruments that flickered in a variety of greens. Then there were the coils that connected dynamo to dynamo, and each pair of dynamos, on either side of the room, to one of two large glass bubbles. If a man wanted to clamber inside and lie down, there was more than enough space for him to do so. He could even take a friend with him; there was ample room. They'd be comfortable; there was cushioning lining part of the bubble. There were also what seemed, even from a distance, like restraints. "A coffin with a view," muttered Eddie.

"What d'you think they're really for?" Bex asked no one in particular.

Lori remembered Frankenstein's gene chamber. "Whatever it's for," she said, "I'll lay odds it's not good."

"You'll get takers for that," Jake said grimly.

There was activity beneath them. They couldn't hear *what* was being said, obviously, but they could see who was saying it.

Gabriel mostly, greeting a black-robed disciple none of Bond Team recognized, a young man who was being physically assisted by several of the Host because he seemed unable to walk straight. He seemed to be laughing a lot, too, as if he found it a matter of great hilarity to have penetrated the sanctity of the Temple of Tranquillity.

Gabriel, the Heavenly Host, and the men and women who sat at the computer consoles were not laughing.

Neither was the woman who entered now. If it was a woman. The figure was so stooped and hunched and leathern with age, like an antique that had been locked in a chest for a hundred years, that it was almost impossible to tell. Her face was the texture of a dead tree, her skull almost bald, a shriveled nut. She wore a single shapeless overgarment.

"See her down there," Bex whispered to Eddie, "that's your girlfriend."

"Yeah?" Eddie retorted. "She's nearly as bald as you are."

"Quit bicker —" Lori changed her command to "Get back!" The disciple was looking up at them directly and enjoying it.

"It's all right," Jake said. "He's drugged or something. No way he'll notice us. Probably doesn't even know where he is, poor sucker."

"Or where he's going," Cally added. But she did. It was becoming chillingly obvious.

The disciple was strapped giggling into one of the glass bubbles — maybe the restraints tickled, those wires at his Temples. The crone helped politely into the other. Someone set the dynamos working. The hum of harnessed energy reached Bond Team even outside the pyramid. Green lights changed their allegiance to red.

The disciple was no longer giggling.

His mouth was still open, though, and gaping wider all the time, like he was trying to unhinge his jaw. Both he and the old woman were arching their backs — hers would surely snap any second like a petrified twig — flapping up and down like fish out of water. Their agonies were silent, but they were agonies nonetheless.

"So this is what passes as missionary work for the Temple of the Transformation," Lori said distastefully.

A mission to the morgue," Cally's hands were fists against the pyramid glass. "They're killing them!"

"I don't think so." Bex shook her hooded head. "This is what they were bidding for, back at the Centennial Club. This is what the old and wealthy wanted."

"What?" Eddie scoffed. "Electrocution in a spiritual environment?"

"'Life is life, Mr. Baxenthorpe,'" Bex recalled, "'and life is what we are offering.'"

"Look!" Jake and Lori together.

The disciple's hair, it was a little difficult to tell from their vantage point, but was it graying, thinning, losing its gloss? It looked that way. And the old woman, hers was spinning from her skull like threads of gold. Her body seemed to be filling out, finding its curves again, her limbs lengthening, strengthening.

Current crackled through the coils between the bubbles. Energy, Bex knew, raw, living energy, and heading in one direction only.

The disciple was doomed.

* * *

"Life transference technology." Ben breathed the words aloud as if to test their reality. "So that was your special project, Mr. Late and Unlamented Nagashima. That's the secret of the Soul Stealer."

The blueprints were in front of him. Life-Force Transfer Units. They looked a bit like bubbles, Ben thought. There had to be two of them, and two subjects at least, one placed in each unit. One to siphon off the vital essence of the first subject, one's vigor and youth and strength, the core of one's continued existence. Siphoned off and carried to the second bubble, using it to revive old bones, tired limbs, to restore health and life and energy to one on the brink of death, to suck the soul from one hapless victim and feed it like medicine to somebody else. Somebody who could and would pay astronomical sums of money to cheat the Reaper, Ben thought, even at the cost of an innocent life.

So the mystery of the psimurai was also solved. It *had* been Hiro Nagashima whom he and Bex had seen at the Centennial Club, an eighty year old man in a body made young again by the evil miracle of life transference technology. And when he and Cally had short-circuited Nagashima at the Pleasure Mall, the energy overload must somehow have reversed or negated the process, aged him half a century in half a second. No wonder he dropped dead. His heart wouldn't have been able to stand the strain.

Ben returned his full attention to the schematics of the Life-Force Transfer Units. Just outlines here, theory. But he knew where the working models would be found.

* * *

"Tell me that was like a special effect," Bex faltered. "Tell me it didn't happen."

"I could tell you, Bex," said Eddie softly, "but I'd be lying."

It was over now. Joy unbridled from the second glass bubble, where a gorgeous blonde woman, perhaps thirty and blessed with the kind of figure men dreamed of, was evidently calling to be released. When she was, how she reveled and luxuriated in her body, like a model on a photoshoot, flaunting herself before her admiring audience.

"You know when I said she was your girlfriend, Ed," said Bex. "I didn't mean it."

Neither Gabriel nor the woman even glanced at the other bubble, but Bond Team did. They watched two Host members open it up and drag out a corpse appropriately robed in black, the husk of a man of at least a hundred, a withered shell, and it seemed as if the disciple had already been decades dead. The sight of him absorbed them in horrified fascination.

A mistake.

Rising on silent wings behind them, a member of the Host closed in.

It was probably best to download everything, Ben thought, the entire Soul Stealer file. Most of it was couched in scientific terms he didn't understand and didn't really want to, but the Spy High techs would lap it up like cats with milk. All those diagrams and blueprints. Ben clicked through them. Nagashima may have been twisted, but he'd also been a genius. Not unlike Dr. Frankenstein before him. There was obviously a thin line between genius and lunacy. A pity so many potentially great men either chose or were somehow persuaded to step over. A thin line between a statue in your honor or a Spy High team on your tail. Ben thought of Uncle Alex and the cliff top all those years ago. Reaching for the sky was good. Wanting the sky all to yourself, now *that* was . . .

What should he have noticed? It was several schematics back. His mind had been drifting, and he'd only subliminally registered the importance of the diagram.

Ben clicked back. There it was. "Gotcha," he grinned.

Designs for a communications center to stage worldwide biddings for life transference treatment. More crucial still, and written in white on black: instructions for installment at the Centennial Club, Boston, U.S.A.

Nagashima hadn't been working alone. This Uncle Alex needed to see.

His reflection gave him away. Jake saw the white-robed man in the glass just in time to yell, "Hoods up!" to the others. If their faces couldn't be recognized, maybe their cover could still be preserved.

"You! Disciples!" It was Peter, not so welcoming now, but luckily for them, if they could only exploit the fact, unaccompanied. "Turn around and don't move."

"At the same time? Might be a bit difficult," Eddie pointed out.

"Turn around, *then* don't move," Peter refined, "or you'll regret it." One hand he kept on his jet pack's control disc, which was at his waist. With the other, he directed a shock blaster at the errant disciples.

Lori could have cursed her foolishness for not having someone keep watch. Ben wouldn't have committed the same error. And now, due to her inexperience, they'd had it.

"What do you think you're doing?" Peter didn't quite seem to believe they were there.

"Couldn't sleep," said Eddie. "Wanted a breath of fresh air."

"Who are you? Take your hoods off. Let me see you." Nobody moved. "Do it!" He sounded nervous more than anything. The inflections in his voice, not those of a stone-cold killer.

So Jake did something else instead. He jumped. He propelled himself from the pyramid with as much power as he could muster and he leaped at Peter, pounced on him like a predator.

It would be fair to say that Peter was not expecting such a sudden and almost suicidal development.

If he'd moved faster, used his blaster, or even flown higher or lower, they'd have been looking for scraps of Jake Daly at the foot of the pyramid for days. As it was, however, shock meant he did nothing, and doing nothing always meant defeat.

Jake had judged his leap perfectly. He rammed into Peter's lower body, found handholds in the Host's robes, gripped tightly, and let his extra weight do its work.

Peter struggled as they started to drop. The jet pack couldn't keep the both of them aloft. He struggled to shake Jake off, pounded at his head with the butt of his shock blaster, but couldn't find the leverage to hurt him. "What are you . . . ? You'll kill us both!" Spiraling out of control. Looping drunkenly toward the lower levels of the pyramid.

Jake snatched at the control disc. A little additional interference with its directional capability couldn't go amiss. The flank of the pyramid flung up to strike them.

He wondered how Peter was going to work out as a safety mat.

By the time the others had scrambled down to his level, Jake had pretty much recovered. He'd also checked that Peter would live, though unconsciously for a good few hours yet.

"Jake Daly, you're a class-A lunatic!" Bex sounded like she approved. "You could have killed yourself."

"Would have saved the Temple the trouble."

"Poor old Peter," sighed Eddie. "Could be a demotion back to the disciples for you."

"It's the least he deserves," Cally glared. Though whether she was referring to his future prospects in the Temple or his present inquiries, Eddie couldn't decide.

"That was reckless, Jake, stupid." Lori's expression was locked into a frown. "And as team leader I have only one thing to say." Then she was smiling. "Good job." Jake's quick thinking had saved them. She wouldn't forget it. "Now let's get back to the dorms. Our mission is still alive, people."

"Oh, no," moaned Eddie. "Does that mean the fields again tomorrow? Peter, man, wake up. I'm surrendering. Name's Enoch . . ."

Ben SkyBiked to his uncle's Maine estate. The mansion was the epitome of Southern elegance transposed to the wilder East Coast, like a refugee Louisiana gentleman from before the Civil War.

"Ben!" Uncle Alex was delighted to see him. "Such a pleasant surprise. Mellors told me to expect you. I assume you'll be staying for lunch."

"I can't think about food right now," Ben said, "and I don't think you'll be hungry, either, after you've seen what I've got to show you, Uncle Alex."

"Indeed? That *does* sound serious." He seemed impressed. "Perhaps we'd better talk in the study."

They did. Ben told Alexander Cain as much as he could without explicitly compromising the security of Deveraux Academy. Did his uncle remember his odd and rather garbled video call from a few days ago? Of course. Well, Ben had learned that one of the men who'd been at the Centennial Club the same night as he and his friend was called Hiro Nagashima. Uncle Alex knew *of* Hiro Nagashima, elderly and Japanese he guessed, but could not recall ever having met him. Ben passed across the plans for the communications center. Well, he'd hacked into Nagashima's computer files and found these. He'd warned Uncle Alex that something was wrong at the Centennial Club, and here was the proof.

Uncle Alex was duly astonished, regarding Ben with new respect. "I don't know what to say," he declared. "But how is it you're privy to such information?"

Ben warmed to Uncle Alex's approbation. "At school," he admitted. "We do have one or two kinds of extracurricular activities."

"Indeed?" Uncle Alex nodded. "You and your friends together, I suppose? The friends who came to your party?"

"You could say that, but I'm trusting you not to, Uncle Alex."

"Of course, Ben, of course." He flourished the sheaf of papers in his hand. "And now, if you'll excuse me, I'd better make some calls to the club. Must ensure my house is in order, as it were. Why don't you stay here and relax for a while? I shouldn't be long."

"Sure," said Ben. "Then maybe I'll be up for some lunch after all."

"Good," said Alexander Cain from the study door. "That's

good. Oh, and Ben," with an appreciative smile, "you've been very helpful."

Just before midday the disciples were gathered at the base of the pyramid. The giant edifice had remained above ground since Bond Team's arrival. It seemed that it only retreated beneath the surface in order to astonish newcomers with its appearance once a week when fresh disciples were brought to Temple Prime. Lori and her teammates did not plan on being around long enough to witness a second performance. Gabriel, too, was apparently only ever seen outside the pyramid to welcome new recruits, and from the platform high above their heads. But he still spoke to his children, daily at noon.

"Couldn't he make it earlier?" Eddie groaned, massaging his joints gingerly. "Then we'd be able to stop work sooner. I'm creaking to death here."

"Do you think he'll mention rogue disciples climbing the pyramid?" Cally asked.

"Maybe." Lori considered. "Peter has to have told him. I'm surprised there hasn't been more evidence of a security crackdown already."

"Maybe he thinks he's got all the angles covered," said Jake. He glanced around him. Above the throng of disciples, the sky seemed slightly thicker than usual with hovering members of the Heavenly Host. If they had to make a break for it, he was thinking, they wouldn't get far. Maybe they should have cut their losses and fled the compound last night.

"Well," Bex said, "at least he doesn't know who we are."

On the wall of the pyramid in front of them, a sequence of

panels lit up, tens of them, the vertical surfaces that faced out toward the Temple's loyal congregation. They extended along nearly the full length of the pyramid from about halfway up to the levels immediately below the glass peak, the Temple of Tranquillity. Together, the panels once activated formed a single screen. And on it, gazing benignly down at his flock with gold-flickering eyes, was revealed Gabriel himself. A reverent hush settled upon the assembled disciples.

"My children," boomed Gabriel, his voice seeming to come from all around them, "what I have to tell you today grieves my heart and troubles my soul. If I could spare you this knowledge, then it would be my duty to do so."

"Don't tell me the World Series has been canceled," Eddie whispered.

"Less talk, Eddie," counseled Lori, "and I think a little more gradually moving backward. I don't like the sound of this."

"There is a serpent in the heart of paradise," Gabriel announced. "There is a stain of sin in the purity of our fellowship." His golden eyes glared. "There are traitors in our midst!"

Instant outrage from the disciples. Bond Team yelled out, too, while at the same time gently easing through the crowd, their black-robed comrades fortunately so consumed with anger that they had little time for observation. But at least Bex was right, Lori reassured herself. Hooded as they'd been, Peter would not be able to identify them even if he was here, which he didn't seem to be.

"Yes, my children," Gabriel was continuing, "our enemies walk among us, those who oppose all we stand for, those dark of purpose who would destroy the harmony of the Temple and deny you all the wonderful gift of Transformation."

"Keep talking, sucker," Jake grunted. "We're nearly there."

The disciples in their urgency were pressing forward. Bond Team was at the margins of the mob. But the Host was circling, probing.

And Gabriel was laughing, suddenly, his humor echoing across Temple Prime like thunder. "But fear not, my children," he consoled. "Our enemies cannot succeed. The false disciples cannot elude the righteous justice of the Temple. They think they are safe, they think they are secret, but the eyes of Gabriel see all. Eyes blessed by the holy powers with true vision. And I tell you truly, my children. The unbelievers stand with you now!"

It seemed the greatest shock of all. Disciple flinched from disciple as if he or she might be one of them.

"Why do I get the feeling he's looking at us?" groaned Eddie.

"I see them, the false disciples." Gabriel's blunt finger jabbed from the screen. "Martha. Mary. Delilah. Enoch. Luke. Surrender now. Admit your crimes. You cannot escape."

"And you know what?" quailed Bex. "He could be right. . . ."

He'd done the right thing, hadn't he? Ben paced the study restlessly waiting for Uncle Alex to return. Now a full internal investigation into the Centennial Club and its membership could be carried out, but quietly, subtly, outside the glare of any negative publicity and the detrimental impact that it might have on the perceived integrity of the club. He'd wanted to protect Uncle Alex from any scandal and he'd done that, hadn't he? And he'd only had to hint at the existence of Spy High.

And if he couldn't trust Uncle Alex, who *could* he trust?

Ben browsed the study shelves. Uncle Alex was taking his time. Lunch? Much longer and they might as well go straight to dinner. Maybe he could leaf through one of the books. Uncle Alex wouldn't mind. Not that they were the most captivating volumes Ben had ever seen, more like the titles reserved for those parts of a library where nobody under the age of sixty ever went. No light reading. No novels at all. Scientific books by writers whose names would be unlikely to trouble the bestseller list.

Lunt. Mazarin. Moberley. Montcalm. Nagashima.

Nagashima.

Ben blinked, but his eyes had not lied. *Energy in the Age of Tomorrow* (English Edition). Nagashima. Ben withdrew the book from the shelf. He opened it. There was a handwritten inscription on the first page. "To my dear friend, Alexander. Those of like mind are destined to work together. Long may we continue to do so. Hiro."

Alexander who? Not Cain. Impossible. Not Alexander as in Uncle Alex. Ben felt his mind slipping. Uncle Alex had never met Hiro Nagashima. He'd told him so. And what on earth could they possibly have worked on together?

Soul Stealer.

"Oh, my God," Ben uttered.

"Not quite, Ben, but one day, who knows? Ambition is everything."

CHAPTER TWELVE

"Let's bypass the usual ritual of shocked protestation, shall we?" said Alexander Cain, eyes glittering like blue ice and gun leveled steadily at Ben's chest. "I'm not sure I could bear all that, 'Oh! Uncle Alex! It can't be you!' and 'I don't believe it!' kind of things. Clichés are so common, aren't they?"

"But . . . but . . ." Ben couldn't even manage a cliché at the moment. His entire brain seemed numb.

"But? Surely you can be a little more articulate than that? Did your parents waste their money on all those elocution lessons?"

"You . . . and Nagashima . . ."

"Were partners, yes, have shared business interests and a certain philosophy toward life for many years. I knew about the Life-Force Transfer auctions at the Centennial Club, of course I did, although I never led any of them myself. Raising money in such a way is so vulgar. Nothing goes on in the club of which I am unaware. Not even the intrusion of a pair of reckless teenagers equipped with the most interesting of gadgets. You must introduce me to your tailor one day, Ben."

"So the communications center we saw . . ."

"We removed it, yes. And let me tell you, it was rather a nuisance having to remodel the communications level so quickly. Nagashima was really quite incensed by it. If he'd known you were responsible, then he'd probably have sought an audience with you sooner."

"But you didn't know —" the irony of it made Ben want to shout "— until I told you." But shouting wouldn't help. He had to regroup his mental defenses, his whole outlook. Uncle Alex had a gun on him. That made him the bad guy. Sixteen years of thinking one way and he had to reverse it in as many seconds. Friend into foe like day into night. He should have listened to Lori.

"Don't be too hard on yourself," sympathized Uncle Alex, as if privy to his thoughts as well as his words. "Mistakes are what help us to learn. Sadly for you, of course, mistakes can also be fatal."

A fresh horror occurred to Ben. "You knew about Nagashima — the psimurai. You sent him to kill me."

"I'm afraid no encouragement was required on my part."

"But . . . you were at my baptism. You've known me since I was . . . I've looked up to you my whole life. How could you even . . . ?" Ben trailed away.

"One has to protect one's interests," sighed Cain, "whatever the cost. That's the first rule of survival in today's brutal world. But if it makes you feel any better, I was rather pleased when I read about the death of an elderly Japanese gentleman in a samurai suit. While attending a costume party in a Pleasure Mall, the report said. I knew it was lying. I knew that you'd somehow bested Nagashima. To cover up the truth so slickly means you must have some powerful friends, Ben."

"Ditto with enemies," Ben noted bitterly.

"Ah, but that's why I'm glad you escaped my late partner. Your resourcefulness has proven that I was right to follow your progress as you grew, right to nurture you and shape you in my own image. There is no need for us to be enemies."

"No need? What about the Soul Stealer? Sucking the life out of somebody and then pumping it into some rich guy makes for a need. It's wrong. It's evil."

"Please, Ben. People like us ought to be beyond the stifling limitations of conventional morality. Life transference technology is simply the latest form of transplant. Before medical science learned how to grow new internal organs in labs, kidneys, hearts, and lungs were transplanted as a matter of course. This is no different."

"It is and you know it." Despite the blaster pointed at him, Ben's fury dared him closer to Cain. "Organ donors had to be willing. People signed things. It isn't the rich exploiting the poor like at your sick auctions."

"Oh, come now. Don't disappoint me with such naïveté after I've just praised your potential. There was always a black market in organ donation. The rich and the strong have always used the poor and the weak for their own purposes. Haven't you understood?" Cain's voice rising with the certainty of one inspired. "That is the single most important lesson I ever taught you. The wealthy have a right to wield their power. We lead where the ignorant masses can only follow. What are a few paltry and anonymous lives compared with those of us destined to be masters of the world? Insects and giants, Ben, insects and giants. And we giants take what we want. No one can stop us."

"Don't you believe it," Ben gritted.

"What? Who, then?" And Ben recognized the unbearable, insufferable arrogance. He sensed it within himself and alongside his anger there was shame. "You? You're going to stop me from the wrong end of a blaster?" Cain grew crafty. "Or perhaps you mean your friends. Perhaps you think they're on the way to accomplishing their mission at Temple Prime."

"Where?" Ben feigned ignorance.

It didn't fool Cain. "The calls I made earlier — there was in fact only one, and it wasn't to the club. I thought if you'd accessed Nagashima's files, you might have uncovered even more about our operation. It seems I was right. Did you know that a number of guests from your sixteenth birthday party are now masquerading as disciples of the Temple of the Transformation? I think you probably did. Well, by now I imagine the masquerade is over."

Ben felt a chill in his heart. "Uncle Alex, what have you done?"

"Oh, no need to panic. I'm sure your friends are quite unharmed. Reasonably sure. Captured, of course, but otherwise quite possibly in the best of health." The consternation on Ben's face amused Cain. "Shall we join them?"

"What's everyone looking so down about? We're inside the pyramid, aren't we? And pretty much in one piece." Though if the Host hadn't been around to pull the enraged disciples off them, Eddie imagined that by now Bond Team would have been in lots of *little* pieces.

"Inside the pyramid, yeah," Jake conceded. "But also inside a cell. I don't think that was quite the idea, Ed."

Eddie looked around him thoughtfully. A toilet in the corner, a kind of bunk made of planks set into one wall, and bars that looked as unbending as Gabriel's will. Not the worst cell he'd ever been incarcerated in, but hardly the Beverly Hills of prisons, either.

"Well, I'm with Eddie," said Cally firmly. "They've left us alive and that's their first mistake. They've left us alone and that's their second."

"Three strikes and we're out?" Eddie rattled the unyielding bars. "Or not."

Cally peered through the bars as well. Beyond, there was a

short corridor that ended at a pair of sliding doors, presently closed. More tempting still, on the far side of the corridor, what had to be the cell door's controls were paneled into the wall. "If we could only reach them," Cally mused.

"It's no good, Cal." Lori slumped onto one of the wooden beds. "*I'm* no good. I'm thinking maybe you should have voted somebody else for team leader." She was thinking that Ben would know what to do in a situation like this.

"Don't be stupid, Lo." Jake was by her side, strong hand squeezing her shoulder comfortingly. "You're the one."

"Jake's right, Lori," Eddie chimed in. "Getting captured and facing certain death — that has nothing to do with you. That *always* happens, whoever's leader. Secret agents going on missions and *not* getting captured and facing certain death is like surfers riding the wave and not getting wet. Capture's not the problem. *Escape's* the problem."

"Speak for yourself, Eddie," Bex said. "Me, I'm out of here."

The others turned toward her, saw her parting her robes to bare her midriff.

"What?" said Eddie. "You're gonna belly-dance your way through the bars, past the guards . . ."

"Not quite." Bex plucked at her navel. "They might have confiscated our clothes and shaved my head, but they left me my piercings. And for the benefit of Cally and Ed —" she presented her small and silver navel stud to her teammates "— that's their third mistake. This baby is not just for show."

Lori was on her feet, sensing hope. "A laser stud," she said.

"Single charge only. But if I can hit the door's control panel from here . . ."

"No ifs, Bex." Lori was adamant. "You've got to."

"I've got to." Bex sighed. "No pressure then."

"You want to let me try, I will." Jake reached out his hand. Bex frowned. Didn't he think she was up to it? Did the others still not entirely believe that she merited her place?

"That's real big-hearted of you, Jake," she said, facing the bars, "but put money on me managing."

One shot. The control panel reading red. Bex lined the stud up, didn't hesitate. A thin beam of white stabbed between cell and wall. It struck the panel dead center. "Bull's eye." Bex grinned. "No need to applaud. Just remember me in your wills." Red stuttered to green and the locking mechanism clicked open.

"Let's go," said Cally.

"Not yet." Lori was planning. "We don't know what's through those sliding doors. If we just burst through now, we'll have the element of surprise but not much else. We could do with some hardware. Something to equalize the odds."

"Do you think there's a take-out ammunitions store we can contact close by?" Eddie wondered.

Lori ignored him. It came with practice. "Jake, by the door. We'll make like the place is burning down or something. When they send someone in, take them out. With any luck, they'll have a little extra on them that we can borrow."

"Gotcha," Jake nodded, "boss." He winked as he darted from the cell.

"All right," Lori said as Jake pressed himself against the wall at the end of the corridor. "Let's give those lungs some exercise."

They shouted. They screamed. The whole pyramid could probably hear them, but it only mattered that one single guard did — heard them and came to investigate.

The doors slid open. A Host member with glaring eyes

stormed through. "What do you think . . . ?" He could count. Four prisoners instead of five. His glare converted to a gape of astonishment.

As Jake fell on him from behind and with a well-placed blow relieved him of his consciousness. Then of his pulse rifle.

"Make sure that's on stun, Jake," Lori said. "Half the Temple is more or less brainwashed. What they're doing isn't really their fault. I don't want unnecessary casualties."

"What about the other half?" muttered Cally, thinking of Mac.

"We secure what's through there as quickly as possible." Lori's eyes were sharp now, bright with determination. "Two teams. Bex and Eddie. Cally and Me. Jake, cover us. Questions? Good. Are we ready?"

The Host members in the prison center control room never knew what hit them. There were only half a dozen of them in any case, not even a decent workout by Spy High standards, and they were expecting Brother Matthias to appear through the doors, not the five teenaged prisoners who'd already caused them so much trouble. Maybe it was that lack of preparedness that made them slow to react. And in a conflict situation, if you didn't react at once, you often didn't get the chance to react at all.

Blasts from Jake's pulse rifle felled two of them as they rose uncertainly from their consoles, sent them spinning backward. Cally and Lori slammed into the two on the right, Eddie and Bex whirled into the pair on the left. Martial arts in textbook flurries. Mr. Korita would have been proud. Objective achieved in seconds. Lori allowed herself a brief and understated smile. Maybe this leadership thing wasn't so bad after all.

"Jake, watch the door." The orders were coming instinctively now, and they felt *right*. "Cally, computer. See if you can rustle up a floor plan, tell us where we are. Eddie, Bex, help me get the Host's robes off."

"Beg your pardon?" Eddie made a face.

"I think we've just earned a promotion."

Bond Team set about its tasks rapidly and single-mindedly.

"We're eight levels below Gabriel's living quarters, according to the pyramid layouts," Cally announced promptly, "and ten below the Temple of Tranquillity itself, up where we were last night. And get this. Those glass bubbles? Life-Force Transfer Units."

"What's in a name?" grunted Jake from the door. "Murder's always murder."

"Good work, Cal," praised Lori. "So we've got two targets and enough Host robes and pulse rifles to go around. We might be a little less conspicuous if we at least *look* like we belong. Cally, while the rest of us are getting changed, send the standard distress call to Spy High. We'll do what we can, but I think we'll need help."

"So what exactly are we going to do?" Jake asked.

"Eddie and Bex are going to pay a little call on the blessed Gabriel," Lori said, "while you, me, and Cally — we're going to burst the Life-Force Transfer Units bubble, once and for all."

Ben was feeling sick to his stomach, though the nausea had nothing to do with his present helicopter flight, the state-of-the-art chopper skimming just inside the atmosphere at almost supersonic speed. He wasn't even upset by the shock blaster that was nuzzling rather uncomfortably between his ribs, held there by a lackey who seemed to find it unnecessary to blink or to look anywhere but at Ben. It was Uncle Alex who'd set his insides churning. Uncle Alex who sat in front of him next to the pilot, who was enjoying the ride like a tourist.

Uncle Alex who'd betrayed him.

And such a betrayal. Ben could scarcely comprehend it. In the last few hours the certainties on which he'd built his whole life had been swept away, had crumbled into dust like the pillars of an ancient Temple. He'd placed an almost religious faith in everything Uncle Alex had ever said. And now, all that was gone, lost — lies. Uncle Alex was now revealed in his true colors, colors that were actually pretty much all black. He was another ruthless, power-hungry madman, like all the others Bond Team had faced.

"I realize it might take you a little while to get used to this." Cain's voice sounded through the headphones but the man himself didn't bother to turn around. "This realignment of our relationship."

"A little while?" Ben retorted bitterly. "Try never."

"Ah, never." Cain chuckled. "Such an endearingly old-fashioned concept. You'll find it difficult to get on in this world if you believe in never as a viable bargaining position, Ben. Right and wrong. Good and evil. They're suits of clothes that we take off or put on at will."

"Yeah? I've never been big on fashion, Cain."

"Cain?" He almost sounded hurt. "What happened to Uncle Alex?"

"That's what I'd like to know."

"Well, perhaps you'll feel differently once you appreciate the true genius of our operation. We should be approaching Temple Prime any moment now. And do try to keep an open mind at least. Ask yourself where your loyalties truly lie. With the lowlifes who infest the globe like lice, ignorant and unthinking, or with the elite social class into which you were born — the pioneers, the leaders. Do you have the courage to join us?"

"Join you?" Ben winced.

"Oh, yes. That is why you're here," Cain explained. "I've decided I owe you the choice, given our past relationship. I've always liked you, Ben, but take care. This will be your one and only opportunity. You either stand with me or against me. Which is it to be?"

Fortunately, Ben's response was postponed by the pilot's announcement that Temple Prime was below them. "Take us down, then," Cain instructed as if to a child. The helicopter dutifully descended. Ben peered out of the window. His vision was first obscured by the cloud but as the chopper dipped lower still, the cloud cover cleared and Temple Prime came into view, the fields, unlikely in the desert, the humble buildings. The pyramid.

They were heading straight toward the side of the pyramid. The very *solid* side of the pyramid.

"Are we, ah, thinking of landing this thing?" Ben ventured.

And then this particular side of the pyramid was *not* so solid. Instead, it split open about halfway down the structure, the wall retracting to reveal a landing bay beyond. Another helicopter was already on the pad.

With consummate skill, enough to earn the slightest nod of approval from Cain, the pilot maneuvered the chopper through the gap and safely into position alongside its companion.

"Welcome, Ben," said Cain, "to Temple Prime."

Ben said nothing. He was also helpless to act right now, the goon with the blaster glued to his side even as they clambered out of the helicopter. But he was thinking of operational possibilities. If the others were here, even if they were captured, they had a chance.

Maybe more than a chance. Here was a guy in white robes rushing anxiously up to Uncle Alex. Anxious usually meant problems and problems for the other side was always good.

"You have something to report, Noah?" Cain's eyes were already narrowing.

"The prisoners, sir . . . they've escaped."

Ben tried to suppress his grin but didn't quite make it.

Cain sighed. "Then find them, Noah, and do it quickly."

"But, sir," dared the lackey, "what if they're not working alone? What if . . . ?"

"Where is your faith, Noah?" Cain reprimanded. "Our friends in the government will protect us as always. Politicians grow old like everyone else. They like to cling to life as well as to power. They will not allow our operation to be betrayed. You see, Ben," he added, turning to him, "nobody really cares about the disappearance of drifters and dropouts. Missing persons are soon forgotten. That is why the Temple will continue to succeed. Now is there anything else, Noah?"

"Only Mr. Baxenthorpe, sir. He's arrived for his treatment."

"Of course he has. Then have him escorted to the Temple of Tranquillity. Oh, and Noah —" as the man was moving off "— when you have apprehended the intruders, have them brought there, too." He regarded Ben with a humorless smile. "Time for our little reunion."

Alarms, Lori reflected. It was surprising how different they could sound. There was the single high-pitched note, sustained like an everlasting scream. There was the chunkier and monotonous honk like an electronic horn. There was the ululating wail as if the villain's complex were suddenly overrun by police cars. The Temple's choice was for a kind of repeated metallic trilling with undertones of menace. But, Lori supposed, the exact nature of the alarm didn't really matter. They all meant the same thing, if you were the reason for them: Watch your back.

"Just look natural," she reminded her teammates as they approached a pair of Host members walking the other way. "We're pure as our robes. We know where we're going."

A nod of greeting as the two groups passed. Nothing more.

"Hope Eddie and Bex are doing as well," Cally said. She noticed Jake and Lori briefly touching fingers. "Maybe I should have gone with them."

"No, we need you with us." Lori was in no doubt. "You're the technowhiz, Cal. We'll need you to put those transfer units out of commission."

"Come on, then," Jake urged impatiently. "The hoods help us, but we don't want to hang around."

"We won't. We're here." Cally indicated an elevator door ahead of them. "Plans said a single elevator dedicated to Temple of Tranquillity access. May I introduce you?"

Jake punched the call button. "You sure may."

"Stay where you are!" Barked from behind.

Jake and Cally were raising their pulse rifles instantly. "No!" hissed Lori, tugging their sleeves. She'd seen. No danger yet. Coming toward them, three Host members escorting a fourth, though this one hanging his head in disconsolate shame. As well he might. It was Peter. Obviously, his painful encounter with Bond Team had done more than blot his record. His record was about to be thrown away, and hapless Brother Peter with it.

"Wait for us," from one member of the Host.

"Of course," Lori said, as emotionlessly as she could. "Elevator's on its way."

"Gabriel wants this incompetent piece of trash taken to Tranquillity," the man informed them. "On a one-way trip to the Life-Force Transfer Units."

"It wasn't my fault," Peter complained desolately. "Please, give me a second chance."

The man shook his head. "Don't know what the Temple's coming to. Hosts who can't do their job and disciples who turn out to be unbelievers. Hear that alarm? They're still on the loose. Could be under our noses right now."

Lori hoped that the elevator would get here very, very quickly.

"Say, you're not techs or anything, are you? Why do you want to go to Tranquillity?"

For the first time, Peter looked up from the floor.

The elevator button blinked that the car had arrived.

"Extra security," lied Lori. "In case the intruders —"

"It's them! It's them!" Through recognition or instinct, Peter was howling. "They're the intruders!"

Now not even Lori could deter Jake. His first pulse blast lifted a Host member virtually off his feet, Cally's spun a second foe around like a drunken ballet dancer.

The elevator doors slid open. Cally backed through them, expecting her teammates to follow. But Peter was hurling himself at Jake, wrestling him to the ground with the reckless strength of a man who has nothing to lose. Lori was dispatching the fourth Host member clinically enough, but now Jake and Peter were rolling on the floor and if she fired, she might hit the wrong one.

"Cally, go!" A fusillade of blasts from farther down the corridor. Host reinforcements. Cally moved forward to help her friends. Blasts crackled around her, forcing her to retreat again.

She saw Lori's eyes, blazing blue. "I said go!"

Team leader's orders. Cally had to go on. She had a mission to complete.

The elevator doors closed on Lori's last stand. Up to the Temple of Tranquillity and the Life-Force Transfer Units.

Cally selected down.

In the Temple of Tranquillity, no alarm could be heard. There was only the slow, sleeping hum of the dynamos, the fussy click of the keyboards, like a grandmother's knitting needles, as techs prepared for a life transference episode. And the dull drone of Alexander Cain.

He was explaining everything, from the basic technology of the Life-Force Transfer Units to the inspiration behind his and Nagashima's creating the Temple of the Transformation to provide suitably unsuspecting and unquestioning subjects for their wider scheme. Ben didn't like it. Gloating time as extended as this could mean only one of two things. Either Uncle Alex was so certain that Ben would never escape the pyramid that it didn't matter, and that was scary. Or, he was convinced that Ben would finally choose him to abandon Bond Team and side with him, and that was probably scarier.

Because what if he was right?

There was activity at the elevator. The white-robed guy called Noah was bustling in, together with a group of about half a dozen of his fellows. And a pair of captives, Ben groaned inwardly.

Cain, on the other hand, seemed delighted. "Ah! The pretty girlfriend and the black-haired boy. I'm *so* glad you could join us, though I suspect our presence here is coming as something as a shock, yes?"

"You're kidding, right?" Jake scowled. "We had you down for a madman from the start, Cain." The Centennial Club connection was fitting into place. One way or another, the mission was building to its climax. The only question in Jake's mind now was about Ben. What would knowing the truth about his precious Uncle Alex do to him? Jake could see the blaster jabbing at him, could see the conflicting emotions on his teammate's face. How was he going to react?

"I *was* expecting your friends to be here as well," Cain was saying.

"They will be, sir," assured Noah nervously. "They won't stay free for long."

"Let us hope you are correct in that assertion, Noah," Cain observed. "For *your* sake."

All this time, Lori had said nothing. Of course, she'd immediately drawn the same conclusion as Jake regarding Cain's involvement with the Temple, and she was little surprised. And of course she felt for Ben, but she hadn't called his name or anything. There was no point. They all knew the score.

Though she was a little perturbed when Cain patted Ben on the back in a friendly, avuncular way, like the blaster wasn't necessary at all, and said: "Well, Ben, the time has come. Choose. Whose side are you on? Will you be true to your breeding, your own kind, to the man who has always had your best interests at heart? Or will you betray your heritage for the sake of a grubby peasant and a girl who cheated on you? I need to know, and I need to know now."

Lori glanced around the room, counted the techs, maybe a dozen enemies, nearly all armed. The chances of fighting their way out of here were minimal. Jake was glowering like a caged animal.

Ben approaching them, his eyes cold, like blue glass, his lip sneering, his bearing arrogant, as if Lori and Jake were beneath him. "Ben?" Lori suddenly felt uncertain.

He struck her across the face, once, with the open palm of his hand.

"Stanton, you piece of —" Jake leaped to attack him, was restrained.

"Ben." It probably wasn't right for team leaders to allow tears to prick their eyes during operational duties, but Lori couldn't help it.

"Oh, well played, sir," chuckled Alexander Cain.

"You turned against me, Lori," Ben said in tones of ice, "but it doesn't matter. It's made my choice easy." He turned his back on her and walked away. "Uncle Alex, I'm with you."

CHAPTER THIRTEEN

Several levels below and several minutes earlier, Eddie and Bex were pondering their own part of the mission.

"You know Gabriel's quarters are going to be guarded, don't you?" Bex pointed out.

"Of course they'll be guarded." Eddie didn't appear troubled by the fact.

"You know we won't just be able to walk right in there and say, 'Okay, Gabriel, hands up. You're coming with us.'"

"As if we would. Without even a please. And Bex? Can you maybe not talk quite so much out of the corner of your mouth? I might be able to understand you a bit better then."

"Eddie!" She was exasperated enough to hit him, probably would have if they hadn't been making their way along what seemed to be a main arterial corridor in the pyramid. They were keeping their progress deliberately slow, deliberately unobtrusive, close to the wall while genuine Host members rushed by, stung into activity by the alarm. "So what's your plan, then? If you've got one."

"Oh, I'm a great believer in the 'don't-panic, something-will-come-along-soon school of spycraft,'" Eddie said from beneath his hood.

"You mean you haven't got a clue."

Eddie's sharp ears picked up the conversation of two members of the Heavenly Host coming toward them. Male and female. Male: key words like "not every member of the Host" and "invited for personal audience with the blessed Gabriel himself." Female: "proud," "honored," and "privileged," punctuated by copious maidenly blushes.

"Wait." Eddie paused while the couple passed by.

"What? Don't tell me you've had an idea."

"Don't panic," grinned Eddie. "Something's just come up. You feeling sexy, Delilah?"

There *were* guards on Gabriel's door, big ones who looked like they'd been hired from the local penitentiary rather than graduated from the ranks of the disciples. They stared at Bex and Eddie suspiciously.

"A little present for the blessed founder," Eddie winked at the guards, "if you know what I mean."

Bex simpered in mock modesty.

"Another one? The last one has only just left."

"Ours is not to question the ways of the blessed Gabriel," Eddie declared offendedly. "Unless, of course, you want me to tell him . . ."

"No, no." The guard cringed despite his size. "I didn't mean anything. Please, go in. Go right in."

"That's better," Eddie nodded. "We will."

As soon as the automatic doors slid shut behind them, Bex did what she'd been longing to do for a while. She slapped her partner. "You enjoyed that, didn't you?" she accused. "Humiliating me out there."

"Well, it got us in here, didn't it? What works, works."

"In here" was a room of sumptuous luxury, thick carpets and deep sofas, indulgent and decadent, like everything was made out of cream. Only one wall threatened to spoil the effect, its monitors, inlaid control panels, and large central video screen apparently having sought refuge here from an office elsewhere.

"Looks like blessed founders live well," Eddie commented.

At which point, the man in question entered from a farther room, lazily draped in silk. "What is it now?" Gabriel began with a kind of spoiled tetchiness. "Yes, you were more than satisfactory, but I told you . . ."

"This isn't an encore, Gabriel." Bex threw back her hood, drew her pulse rifle from the folds of her robes. "It's a whole new show."

"Congratulations, Ben." Alexander Cain pumped his hand vigorously. "Congratulations, indeed. You've made the right decision."

Ben flicked a glare at his former teammates. "The only decision," he said. "It's taken me awhile, Uncle Alex, but I think for the first time in a long time, I can see clearly. I know what I've got to do."

"That's very pleasing." Cain gestured to the lackey with the shock blaster. "Do forgive me, however, if I have my associate Mr. Kyle keep you under close scrutiny for a little while longer. Just in case you suffer a sudden relapse in loyalty. You understand, don't you, Ben?"

"Sure. But you needn't worry, Uncle Alex. I know whose side I'm on."

"Yeah, and so do we, don't we?" Barbed and venomous. It was surprising that Jake had managed to keep quiet this long. "You're a lousy traitor, Stanton. Next time I get my hands on you, I'm gonna tear you apart!"

"Next time?" Cain found the idea amusing.

"Ben, think." Lori was pleading rather than angry. "Think about what you're doing."

"Oh, I am, Lori," Ben said stonily. "Uncle Alex, what's going to happen to them?"

"Why?" Cain probed. "Not concerned for your ex-friends' welfare, I hope."

"Of course not. It's just that whatever you're going to do, I'd like to watch."

Uncle Alex burst into laughter and clapped Ben on the back. "That's what I like to hear. You're a boy who takes after my own lack of heart. I knew you would be, given the right encouragement."

He looked as if he was about to go on before the elevator doors swished open to announce more arrivals. *Not Bex and Eddie,* Lori prayed. *Don't let them be captured, too. Or Cally. Where* was *Cally?* She could tell from Jake's anxious expression that he was thinking the same things. Some relief, then, when no Bond Teamer was escorted from the elevator. The man who now tottered into the Temple of Tranquillity, accompanied by a female member of the Host and incongruously dressed in white slippers and a bathrobe, like he was on his way to the shower, was about as old as the Spy High students combined and then some. A gambling man could certainly have taken bets on whether he'd last long enough to make Alexander Cain's side: It was likely to be close.

"Mr. Baxenthorpe!" Cain hailed. "A pleasure to see you again, and looking so well."

Shriveled lips peeled back to expose naked gums in a dead man's grin. The life transference process was obviously not facilitated by the presence of dentures in its recipient. "I'll look better soon, I trust, Cain," said Mr. Baxenthorpe. "Fifty years better. Unless this alarm I've been hearing means there are rabble-rousers disrupting your organization."

"The situation, Mr. Baxenthorpe," assured Cain, indicating Lori and Jake, "is entirely under control. Everything is in readiness for your treatment."

"Good," Baxenthorpe scowled. "Let's get on with it, then. I might not be here tomorrow. Now," he peered with pensioner's myopia at the Host around him, "which strong, virile, and healthy young person here is going to be privileged enough to give up their life for mine?"

Most eyes turned to Peter. He'd been part of the group who'd brought Lori and Jake to the Temple of Tranquillity, hoping that his role in their capture might have redeemed him for his earlier failure. At the moment, that didn't seem likely.

"No! No! You can't!" He didn't bother with self-respect or pride. Instead, he flung himself straight at Cain's feet and groveled as if his life depended on it. Which, of course, it did. "I recognized the intruders! Without me they'd have got away. I'm loyal, Mr. Cain! Please . . ."

"Noah, is this true?" Cain asked. Noah had to concede that it was. "Then perhaps it *would* be more fitting for another to undergo the marvel of final Transformation."

"Oh, thank you. Thank you, thank you, thank you." Peter would probably have kissed Cain's boots had the man not then stepped over him.

"Another," Cain mused. "Or *others*." He regarded Ben with a sadistic smile. "In answer to your previous question, Ben, I'll tell you what's going to happen to your troublesome friends." He snapped orders to the Host and his voice was like iron. "Put them in the Soul Stealer."

* * *

"You're insane, both of you." Gabriel's analysis of their mental state left Bex and Eddie unmoved. "All I have to do is call out. My guards will rush in, and you'll be cut to pieces."

"Maybe," said Bex, "but not before you take a one-way trip to that temple in the sky yourself."

"I don't know, Bex," pondered Eddie. "Maybe he'd like that. I think there's a nice comfy sofa exactly like this one just waiting for him up there in paradise. I think it's got his name on it already. 'The blessed Gabriel.' Let's send him up there early. I think we'll be doing him a favor. What do say we find out?"

"All right! All right!" Gabriel's defiance did not extend to facing down two pulse rifles. "What do you want? Who *are* you?"

"It doesn't matter who we are," Bex said. "What we *want*, on the other hand . . ."

"See, Calvin — can I call you Calvin? Blessed Gabriel's so formal somehow, isn't it? See, Calvin, we're not entirely happy with this little outfit you're running here." Eddie shook his head and tutted. "It's all a pile of something smelly, isn't it? What's the word? A fake. A sham. A fraud. A cheat. A big, fat, steaming lie is what I think I'm saying, Calvin. You know, like your name, like the Transformation you promise to those poor schmucks in black downstairs."

"We've seen what Transformation really is, Gabriel," said Bex. "It's what people get put in prison for. We'd like to put you in prison for it."

"But first," added Eddie, "my old gran always used to say honesty was the best policy. Never did her any good, but maybe it'll be different for you, Calvin, seeing as how you're so religious to start with and everything."

"What are you talking about?" Gabriel demanded irritably.

"In his own rather roundabout way," Bex clarified, "my partner's talking about the broadcast we want you to make to the whole of Temple Prime." She indicated the videoscreen on the wall. "I'm assuming this is where you transmit your tedious daily sermons? Only what we've got in mind is likely to cause a little more of a stir than the usual."

"Stir? What do you mean?" Gabriel's eyes widened.

"You're going to tell your disciples the truth," said Eddie. "Everything. About you. About what goes on in those glass bubbles. The Temple of the Transformation ends here."

Gabriel gaped. "But I can't. It's impossible. If I do that, the disciples will turn against me. They might even try to harm me!"

"If you *don't* do it," Bex warned, "they won't be the only ones. Eddie, fix the door. We don't want to be disturbed while Gabriel speaks with his adorning public."

"Yes, ma'am." Eddie fired a single pulse blast. It shattered the doors' control mechanism. Now the guards would have to physically pry them open if they wanted in, and that would take time.

Time enough for a little more pulse rifle persuasion if necessary.

"Please. Be reasonable." Gabriel was beseeching now, humble, far from the all-powerful icon at the summit of the pyramid. "None of this is my fault. I'm not to blame. The life transferences, the Temple itself, other people's ideas. I'm just an actor playing a part."

"Then you'll know how to deliver your lines, won't you?" Bex activated the videoscreen. Outside, she knew, one wall of the pyramid would be converting itself into a similar screen. It wasn't midday. Gabriel wasn't supposed to broadcast now. The disciples would sense that something out of the ordinary was happening. They would come running from the fields to gaze on the image of the Chosen One and hang on his every word.

Bex doubted they'd like what they heard.

"Now," she instructed the actor called Calvin Johns. "Talk."

Sometimes, Cally knew from studying strategy and tactics, you had to take one step back now to take two steps forward later on. Or, in terms more dimensionally relevant to her present situation, sometimes you had to go down to go up.

Her pulse rifle slung across her back, she climbed the rungs that pierced the inner skin of the pyramid like safety pins.

When it was obvious that Lori and Jake were going to be recaptured, it was also obvious that the Host would be expecting her to continue to make for the Temple of Tranquillity. A white-robed welcoming committee would certainly be waiting. So Cally did what she hoped qualified as *un*expected. She traveled downward, to the lowest levels reached by the elevator, then she took the maintenance stairways lower still until she was beneath the body of the pyramid itself, where she imagined only techs and engineers ventured.

It seemed like the center of the earth compared with where she was now — clinging to the rung securely and pressing herself against the solid, slanting steel wall, Cally glanced below her. The shaft was black and bottomless.

Among the gears and engines that raised and lowered the mighty pyramid, she'd found what she'd been looking for: access to the structure's inner skin or wall. Externally, the pyramid was ledged and tiered, but internally what seemed to be the outer walls were smooth, meaning that there must be a space between the false exterior and the actual one, a space that maybe extended all the way up to the Temple of Tranquillity.

Above her, remote like a constellation of stars, panels of light rimmed the darkness.

She felt that she'd been climbing for a long time. Her limbs screamed for relief. It was tempting just to hang there, to let the blackness wash over her like midnight seas and wait until somebody found her.

But she had to push on. There was still a mission to complete, and all the while even one member of Bond Team was at liberty, there remained a chance that the mission could be accomplished.

Cally hauled herself higher and wondered what awaited her on the other side of those distant panels.

They struggled, of course, but it did no good. The members of the Host were too many and, besides, Ben's betrayal had knocked some of the protest out of them, particularly Lori.

She and Jake were fastened inside one of the Life-Force Transfer Units.

Gazing at them with a face devoid of emotion, Ben felt Alexander Cain patting his shoulder. "How often is it that young sweethearts claim they want to spend the rest of their lives together?" he said wistfully. "Well, your friends can count themselves fortunate. In a few moments, they'll be able to do precisely that."

"Are we making progress then, Cain?" croaked Mr. Baxenthorpe. "If I'm not reinvigorated soon I'm going to need my pills."

Uncle Alex whisked away from Ben to mollify the old man

and assist him toward his own unit. Mr. Kyle, however, stayed close by. Ben smiled at him innocently to suggest there was no need. Mr. Kyle's lack of response suggested he thought otherwise.

Ben looked across to Uncle Alex and Baxenthorpe. Eyes didn't quite make it. Diverted instead by the Host called Noah, whose blanching expression and sudden outburst of "What? *What?* Are you sure?" presumably prompted by an earpiece communication with someone somewhere else, suggested a problem of significant proportions.

Cain heard Noah, too, paused with Mr. Baxenthorpe not yet in the unit. "What is it?" he demanded.

Noah didn't seem entirely certain. "It's Gabriel," he managed. "Johns has gone mad."

"Mad? Explain."

"He's . . . apparently, he's broadcasting to the disciples. He's telling them the Temple is a lie, that he's an actor employed to deceive them. He's telling them *everything.* . . ."

"Then silence him," Cain snapped quickly. "By whatever means necessary."

"I'm afraid —" and Noah did look a little like it "— he's locked himself in his rooms. The Host is trying to break the door down but . . . there's something else . . ."

"Now is not the time to keep me in suspense, Noah," glowered Cain.

"The disciples. Johns is creating panic." Noah seemed to be sharing it. "They're confused, milling around. There's no telling what they'll do."

"The Host must maintain order at all costs," Cain demanded. "Take your men with you and ensure that it happens,

Noah. Nothing must be allowed to disrupt operations here, do you understand? I hold you personally responsible."

"Yes, sir." Noah did not look happy as he gestured to his fellow Host. "You heard Mr. Cain."

They rushed to the elevator and piled inside, leaving only a handful of techs, Cain, Baxenthorpe, Kyle, and Ben at liberty in the Temple of Tranquillity. If they'd still been free, too, Jake and Lori would now have their chances of staying that way.

"Is this what you call a situation under control, Cain?" carped Baxenthorpe. "Not even able to manage your own puppets. Your organization's a shambles, man."

"Is that right, Mr. Baxenthorpe?" Cain glared at the quivering skeleton before him, seemed to be selecting which limb to pluck off, like a boy with a spider.

"In my day this would never . . . ," Baxenthorpe interrupted by a cough. "In my day . . ." And again. "In . . ." And this time, he didn't stop, wracked by a fit of coughing that made his brittle bones rattle. "Cain . . . Cain . . ." Groping for help.

A single second. In the spy game, sometimes you had to cram a lot in to a single second.

Case in point: Cain bent toward the ailing Mr. Baxenthorpe, and Kyle's steady scrutiny flickered that way, too. Ben had been waiting and now he kicked out with sudden, startling force, sending the shock blaster flying from Kyle's hand. Almost instantly, he was diving for it, grasping, rolling, on his feet, crouching, aiming.

The dynamos' controls were a target big enough to hit even if he had Mr. Baxenthorpe's eyesight, and at Spy High a student's vision had to be 20/20. Ben's first shot demolished one computer and scattered techs in a shower of sparks.

Sadly for him, one shot was all he got.

Kyle was quick, too, rocky fists slamming down on Ben's back like a landslide. For another single second, the world turned red. When normal colors were restored, Ben was on the floor, and the re-armed Kyle and Uncle Alex were standing over him, the latter shaking his head with sorrowful acceptance, as if having heard of the death of a friend after a long illness.

"Oh, dear," he sighed. "Ben, Ben, Ben. So you turn against me after all. And I had such plans."

"You want to know what I think of your plans, Uncle Alex?" Ben raged. "It won't take long. Most of the words have only four letters."

"I'd save your breath if I were you," Cain advised. To the techs: "Damage report. Can the transference still take place?"

"We could bypass console three and boost the power cores if . . ." a tech began.

"I don't want jargon. Yes or no?"

A nervous yes.

"Then do it."

"Help me into the unit, Cain," wheezed Mr. Baxenthorpe, who seemed at least partially to have recovered from his fit. "I feel faint."

"I'm afraid, Mr. Baxenthorpe," said Cain, "your treatment has been temporarily postponed."

"What? You can't! I paid good money . . ."

Cain swept the old man away with his arm. "Temporarily. Postponed." Baxenthorpe collapsed on the floor like a sack of potatoes. "There's another, more pressing matter I must deal with first." His eyes were as cold as death. "Isn't that right, Ben?"

* * *

"Not so clever now, are we, hmm?" The battering on the doors. "Not so witty and wisecracking now." Dents in the steel. "You've had it, you hear me? When the Host get in here —"

"You'll be our shield, Gabriel," said Bex, silencing him with a jab of her pulse rifle.

"Yep. And our ticket out of here as well," contributed Eddie. "You're having a real useful day, aren't you, Calvin?"

"Don't call me Calvin," whined Gabriel. He looked like he was going to say something else, too, but the explosion from the doors took them all by surprise.

The guards had called up reinforcements of the incendiary variety.

All three occupants of the room were thrown backward by the force of the detonation. The doors were punched through like paper and now numbers of the Host could enter. A fusillade of pulse rifle blasts, stabbing furniture and shattering the video-screen, announced their intention to do so.

Eddie sought immediate cover behind a sofa that probably cost more than most people's annual income. Maybe the advancing Host would be careful about damaging it. It wasn't. Pulse blasts ripped into the plump cushions and plush upholstery. "This is gonna have to be paid for!" Eddie yelled, and returned fire.

Bex's instinct was also to protect herself, but they'd have a better chance of doing that if they also had Gabriel. He was scrambling to his feet just a grab's distance from her. She clutched for him. "Oh, no, you —"

He did. From somewhere, Gabriel found the strength to beat off Bex's lunge and to stagger forward out of her reach, toward the Host. "Don't shoot!" he cried. "It's me, Gabriel, the

Chosen One! I'm on your side!" But the actor who'd once been plain Calvin Johns ought to have remembered. The audience can love you. The audience can hate you. But before you go out onto the stage, you never know which one it'll be. "No! Don't . . ."

They did.

"Can we get a refund on that ticket out of here?" grumbled Eddie.

Bex joined him now in creating a crossfire that was causing unconscious Host bodies to pile up, but their number seemed inexhaustible. Even with the advantage of cover, Eddie reasoned, sooner or later they'd be overrun. And then, scorching his skin as the sofa erupted in flame, there wasn't *even* the advantage of cover. And the Host's pulse rifles didn't seem to be set on stun.

Where was a miracle when he needed one?

"Stop!" A barked command, instantly obeyed by the Host.

Could qualify. On the other hand, maybe it was just delaying the inevitable.

Eddie and Bex exchanged desperate glances as the man called Noah joined his comrades.

The dynamos hummed and pulsed in readiness. The coils between the Life-Force Transfer Units glittered like steel cobras. From the wide-eyed urgency on Jake and Lori's faces, Ben could tell that they knew how close they were to having their strength sucked out of them. And they could do nothing about it. They were helpless. Their lives were in Ben's hands and Ben's hands alone. No wonder they felt a little clammy right now.

The techs awaited Cain's command to begin the transfer sequence, though this time the captives' energy was not destined for an occupant of the second unit.

Alexander Cain had removed his jacket and shirt to reveal a garment that could have graced the catwalk in one of Paris or Milan's more surreal fashion shows. It banded his torso and upper arms in black streaks of metal, like the stripes of tigers Ben had seen in the *Extinct Species Guide*, clinging tightly to his body, accentuating the already impressive musculature. The key physical points, the biceps and triceps, above the heart, were embellished by circular pads. Ben didn't know precisely what they were for, but he could guess.

"An exoskeleton," Cain explained. "Another brainchild from the late Hiro Nagashima. The limitation of life transference technology originally, you see, was that its beneficiaries always had to come here for their treatments, and one or two of them tended to get a little squeamish at the sight of their donors shriveling before their vastly improving sight like old fruit. So Nagashima developed this as a kind of portable and more stylish alternative to the units. Life essences can be stored in the dynamos and then transferred to order to the wearer of the exoskeleton via the suit's internal circuitry. A program of mild booster treatments can also be highly beneficial to the health as you can see from my own physique."

"Sorry," Ben sought clarification, "am I supposed to be interested?"

"I think you will be," smirked Cain, "because one other asset of the exoskeleton is that once activated, it uses a donor's life essence to increase and enhance the natural strength of its wearer. To show you what I mean, we're going to have a little demonstration, Ben, and I'm afraid it's your friends who are going to provide my power. I expect that makes you angry, doesn't it, Ben? Do you feel mad?"

"You don't want to know how I feel," scowled Ben.

"Then you must fight me, mustn't you?" said Alexander Cain. "I can see that you want to. Defeat me while I wear the exoskeleton, and your friends will go free. Fail, on the other hand, and you will join them in the Soul Stealer to provide the ailing Mr. Baxenthorpe with his second flush of youth. What do you say, Ben?"

"How do I know I can trust you?"

"You don't, of course." The hint of a smile that reminded Ben of years now lost. "And one last thing. The energy consumption of the suit increases according to need, so the longer our battle goes on, the greater the toll on Lori and Jake."

"Then we'd better get it over with," Ben gritted.

And attacked.

Speed was the essence, speed and swiftness. Take Uncle Alex out before he could react, before the suit was even functioning. Bit of a cheat, really, but playing by the rules didn't always save lives.

Ben's precision kick cracked into Cain's jaw, snapped his head sideways. Cain staggered but managed to activate the suit as he reeled from a second and third kick, staggering, floundering. Ben didn't pause. Maybe he could finish this at once.

The monitors at the dynamos switched to red. In the Life-Force Transfer Unit, Lori and Jake arched their backs in agonized unison.

Uncle Alex was tottering, even as his suit seemed to crackle with life. Ben pressed his advantage, lashed out with another kick, a blur of movement.

But not as fast as Cain's. Hands raised at superhuman speed. Gripped Ben's right ankle, twisted.

Adapt. Use your enemy's moves against him.

Ben rolled in the air, brought his left leg around to strike the side of Cain's head once more. This time, the blow was absorbed like water into a sponge. It did, however, loosen the man's hold on Ben's ankle and allow him to wrest it free, to crouch on the floor, to rally his resources.

Then Cain rammed into him like a juggernaut, like an avalanche, the suit tingling with electricity. Ben was swatted across the room.

"There," laughed Cain. "I'm beginning to feel a little better now, though I doubt you can say the same, Ben, can you?"

It was like everything was made of glass and on the point of shattering. Ben saw in the Soul Stealer: Lori's hair was somehow growing long again, like rich wheat in need of harvest. He saw Cain advancing toward him, too close for kicks.

On his feet again, Ben delivered a barrage of blows. All that Mr. Korita had taught him condensed into five seconds of blistering assault.

But it was like trying to level Mt. Everest with a single stick of dynamite.

And he couldn't evade Cain's eventual response. The fist caught him, knocked him down again. Reduced him to gazing up at Uncle Alex again. It had to stop.

Somehow.

"And so, Ben," chuckled Cain humorlessly, "are you ready to say uncle?"

A sudden explosion erupted from over by the dynamos. Cain instinctively turned his head. Ben didn't. The good spy fought in silence. He threw himself at his foe again.

Cally emerged from the hole in the floor where a glass panel had been. She assimilated the scene faster than the techs or Kyle could assimilate her arrival. Enemies carrying weapons were your first priority. She dropped Kyle with a single pulse blast. Any potential hostiles were your second. The startled techs were stunned except for one. Cally thought she might need him.

"Cal!" Ben yelled as he tried to deflect Cain's crunching fists. "The unit!"

Inside, Lori and Jake were far past retirement age for secret agents, the quick years wrinkling them, hastening them toward their final moment, decades before its time.

Quite how Ben and Alexander Cain had got here Cally didn't know. But they *were* here, and it looked like Cain was the bad guy. Ben was engaging him in hand-to-hand combat, too close for her to get a shot. But she could see Cain's exoskeleton. The indicators on the monitors seemed to synchronize with every blow he made, suggesting that the suit's power was coming directly from . . .

Cally knew she'd been right to keep one tech conscious.

The man cowered before her pulse rifle. "Can the transference process be reversed?" she demanded. It wouldn't be good enough merely to stop it. That would leave Lori and Jake as premature elderlies. "Can it?"

"We could arrest the system at the console and then refigure the polarity . . ."

"Yes or no?"

A nervous yes.

"Then do it."

"No!" croaked a little old man, hobbling toward Cally on skeletal legs. "I won't be cheated. . . . You can't do it . . ."

Wheezing, slowing, parchment eyelids fluttering like leaves in autumn. "I'll make it . . . worth your while. . . ."

Cally wondered whether she might need to use a pulse blast. She didn't. The old man collapsed out of his own accord. All this excitement. Looked like he needed his sleep.

And the tech was good. Suddenly, the dynamos were humming a different note. In the unit, Lori and Jake were aging no further. The years were surging back.

Alexander Cain sensed it. "What? No . . ." He felt the power leaking from his exoskeleton. He knew what that meant.

So did Ben.

His own combinations began to hurt again. He was fighting flesh and blood once more. Cain tried to make a move for Cally and the tech. Ben did not allow it. "I've just got one thing to say," he announced, "before we bring your little game to an end, Uncle Alex." The name punctuated by twin karate chops to either side of the neck. Cain reeled. "That day on the cliff, that reach-for-the-sky day, my sixth birthday. Remember that, Uncle Alex? Of course you do."

"Stand . . . still . . ." Cain flailed but he was slower now, feeling his age. Couldn't connect.

"I believed in you then, you know that?" Ben immobilized Cain, numbing nerve centers with polished efficiency.

"Betray me, Ben," gasped Alexander Cain, "and you betray your whole life."

"No," snapped Ben. "You've *lied* to me my whole life. You were lying then, and you're lying now. All that you stand for, Uncle Alex, the entire sick, exploitative system you represent, it's all lies. It's all lies, and it's all over." With one final tap, hardly more than that, he dropped Cain to his knees. "I used to look up to you, Uncle Alex, but now?" A thin, bitter smile. "Now I'm looking down."

"Ben, that's enough." It was a gentle, calming voice he knew.

"Lori?" Restored. As young as ever. As gorgeous as ever. As if she'd never screamed her life away in the Soul Stealer. She'd been returned intact, but not to him.

"You did good, Ben." Jake, too, in full, tangle-haired vigor.

"Hey, guys. Guys!" Cally's urgency drew their attention smartly. She was pointing to the elevator doors. A car was arriving.

Wearily, Bond Team braced themselves. What if it was packed with armed Host members, loyal to Cain? What if its mission wasn't over yet?

The doors slid open. Two white-robed figures stepped out.

"What? And they told us this floor had soft furnishings," said Eddie.

CHAPTER FOURTEEN

The cleanup operation was well underway.

Army helicopters hovered above the pyramid. Soldiers swarmed over it like ants. The Heavenly Host was led away while black-robed disciples milled around in confused groups. Corporal Keene and certain other personnel linked to Spy High were also present, casting a secretive yet supervisory eye over all.

"Wonder what they're going to do with this now?" Bex nodded toward the pyramid. She and Eddie were talking to Cally in the grounds of Temple Prime. "Could turn it into a tourist attraction, I guess, a themed hotel, maybe. It worked in Vegas."

"Do you mind, Bex?" Eddie said. "I was in the middle of explaining to Cally how we escaped certain death in Gabriel's quarters."

"Exposition Eddie hits his stride again," said Bex. "Excuse me if I go and fall down over here for a bit."

"So you see, Cal," continued Eddie, imperiously ignoring Bex, "seems this Noah guy had looked at the way things were going and decided the Temple's days just might be numbered. So he did the only thing a mercenary scumbag *would* do under the circumstances."

"What's that, Eddie?" said Cally.

"Change sides. Guess he's hoping the courts'll go easy on him when all this comes to trial. Bit of a pity in one respect, though," Eddie added sorrowfully.

"Yeah?"

"I was really looking forward to battling my way to the rescue."

Not far away, near enough for them to hear, came the sound of Bex snorting.

Lori and Ben hardly dared to look at each other. It was like they were on a shy first date, not wishing to offend, not knowing what to say.

"Sorry." Lori finally broke the awkward silence. She *was* team leader, after all.

"Sorry?"

"Yeah. Really."

"Really, why?"

"Everything."

"Oh," said Ben. "Everything."

"You want an example?"

"Could help."

"I'm sorry for doubting you back there, *up* there. I should have known you were only playing along, waiting for a chance."

"Yeah," Ben accepted. "Should have known."

"So I'm sorry."

"Well, you can cross that one off your list, Lo. If anything, it should be on mine." Ben frowned. "The way I've treated you since we split up, the things I said when we did, then stupidly fighting with Jake, and you knew how I worshipped Uncle Alex, it's not surprising you might have started wondering . . ."

"What'll happen to . . . Uncle Alex now?"

A shrug. "Penal satellite, I guess. I don't care. As long as he's kept as far away from me as possible."

"Not talking about me, I hope." Jake couldn't let Lori out of his sight for a moment, could he? Not, Ben sighed inwardly, that he could blame him.

"No, he wasn't," said Lori promptly, "but I'm glad you're here,

Jake. I'm glad you're both here. I want you to end this ridiculous feud between you two right here and now. The team can't afford it, two of its members constantly sniping at each other, but it's not only that. You're the two boys I care about most in . . . well, you know. You both mean a lot to me, and it kills me if I think you can't be friends."

"I guess we can." Jake looked steadily at Ben, extended his open hand. "What do you say, Ben? Let bygones be bygones and all that?" And Stanton wasn't really so bad, after all. It must have taken guts to confront Cain like he did.

"Okay," Ben reciprocated. "You're on." Their hands clasped. "But if you do anything to hurt Lori . . ."

"No chance," said Jake.

They left him alone then. Jake had come over because apparently Corporal Keene wanted a verbal report from Lori as to recent events in her capacity as team leader of Bond Team. Ben remembered the requirement well.

"Ben?" Cautiously.

"Hi, Cal."

"I'm not intruding or anything, am I?" She wasn't. Ben could keep his moping for later. "I've been watching the disciples. Have you seen their faces?" Ben hadn't, not really. "They're all so vacant, so lost. And they're all just kind of shuffling around. They don't know what they're doing. They don't know where they're going."

"I know the feeling."

"That's the worst thing about organizations like the Temple." Cally's tone hardened momentarily. "They create dependency. You rely on them, you trust them, and then they let you down."

"Like people," Ben said. "People can be like that, too."

"Cain," Cally guessed. Paused. "We've both lost somebody close to us, Ben, in different ways. Mac's dead. Your Uncle Alex. We've both got to cope."

"Yeah?" Ben looked at Cally sadly, tiredly. She could have added Lori if she'd wanted. "So how do we do that?"

"We find strength," Cally said. "In ourselves. We find our own way."

And he almost smiled. There was something about Cally's earnestness, something about the way her nose wrinkled up when she grew animated, that he almost smiled. "You know, Cal," he said, "you could be right."

It was several weeks after the team's showdown in the Temple pyramid, a day that could prove every bit as significant, if not more so. It was a day the second year students had dreaded since perhaps the moment they'd joined Spy High: final examinations.

By tomorrow they'd either be graduates, qualified to undertake any and all missions around the world. Or they'd wake up and not even recall the existence of Deveraux Academy — mind-wiped, failed, rejected.

Ben hated the sound of all three of those words.

He gazed up at the austere gothic façade of the school building. It seemed haughty, somehow, aloof, as if it deigned not to notice someone as unimportant as Benjamin T. Stanton Jr. Ben remembered what he'd thought the first time he'd set eyes on Spy High. *I'll make you notice me,* he'd vowed. *I'll prove myself to you, to everyone.* He'd come out here this morning to remind himself of that.

But he couldn't stay. Bond Team's warning bell rang throughout the building. It was time.

So one final moment of reflection and then inside. Past Violet Crabtree's desk where she probably called out good luck or more likely made some comment that in her day, exams were harder. Past the smiling holographic students who didn't have to worry about exams at all, only whether the power was still going. Into the study elevator.

The warning bell sounded again, more impatient now, as if it had something else to do.

Through the high-tech gleam of Spy High corridors. Past

the rec room. Past the IGC. Past two years' worth of memories and dreams.

To the examination center.

The others were there before him.

"Thought maybe you'd had a better offer, Ben," joked Jake, but nervously. "Good luck."

"You, too." Perhaps surprisingly, he meant it.

"I'd wish you luck, too, Ben." Lori squeezed his hand. "But you won't need it."

He hoped. "Wish me it anyway. And you're gonna pass this so easily, Lo."

Eddie and Bex were already in their seats, and Cally, too. She smiled across to Ben as if she felt he needed her reassurance. Maybe he did. "Now I know how they used to feel on the planks," gulped Eddie. "Any last requests?"

"Yeah," grunted Bex. "Shut up."

Then Ben was on his own, making himself comfortable in the leather examination chair, checking that the armrest controls were functioning correctly. How many times had he practiced these tests? He hadn't redlined since they'd returned from Temple Prime. His marks across the board had been steadily rising again. The crisis was passed.

He *hoped* the crisis was past. The next hour would tell.

"Lowering cyberhelmets," said Senior Tutor Grant.

After Uncle Alex, after Lori, after the team leadership, he couldn't lose his place at Spy High as well.

"Good luck, Bond Team," said Grant. "You have sixty minutes."

The strap beneath his chin. The visor across his eyes.

Ben took a deep, determined breath.

"Begin."

Turn the page for a sneak peek at

SPY HIGH:
MISSION SIX

THE ANNIHILATION
AGENDA

Arriving June 2005 from
Little, Brown and Company

Before July 1, 2064, of all the employees at Solartech's Californian plant only one had ever made the national news.

Joel Shuman had been the blue-eyed boy of American athletics for a time. He'd been able to run the 100 meters like he was a blur on the track, like a special effect in a movie, leaving his opponents limping in his wake like old men waddling for their pensions. On his eighteenth birthday, Joel Shuman became the youngest man in history to break nine seconds for the hundred. His future glory seemed assured. Sadly, on the day *after* his eighteenth birthday, Joel Shuman went drinking. Then he went driving. There was an accident. One fatality. Joel Shuman's athletics career. In those days, it was still illegal to compete with a bionic leg.

So Joel's fifteen minutes of fame ended exactly on time. Tales of past triumphs and endless what-might-have-beens didn't put food in his mouth or a roof over his head. He found it hard to get a job, more difficult still to keep one. He'd only ever wanted to be an athlete. Finally, the personnel manager of Solartech, California, who remembered Joel from fading newspaper photographs, before the three-dimensional spreads you could get nowadays, hired him as a security guard. That made Joel's day. (It also numbered them, not that anyone knew it at the time).

Joel Shuman became just another member of the faceless, fameless workforce at the giant Solartech plant — people who had grown resigned to earning their pay, living their lives and dreaming their dreams, believing that the attention of the world had passed them by forever.

All that changed on July 1, 2064.

It was a normal day, to start with: gossip, banter, night shifts leading off, day shifts leading on. Plans for the evening, tomorrow, next week. Small plans, family plans, nothing the press would ever want to know about. Plans that would never be realized.

The explosion occurred at 11:30 AM. The first the workers knew of it was the plant's alarm system shrieking into life, like a woman threatened with a knife. Several of them probably thought it was a drill, and were likely quite affronted when the flames gushed through the corridors like an orange flood and incinerated them where they stood. Others, perhaps those with a little latent psychic ability, must have realized what was happening, what it meant. Perhaps these had time to scream, or to whimper, or to picture loved ones a final time in their minds, or to reach out to clasp whoever was close. It didn't really make any difference.

And Joel Shuman, in his uniform, at the gates? Perhaps he ran. When he heard the roar, when he saw the concrete shatter and the fireball flare, perhaps he ran. He must have thought he had a chance. In his day he'd been able to outsprint anything. But not this time.

Joel Shuman's face appeared alongside all the others on the evening news, his name listed with everyone else's.

A kind of fame had come at last to Solartech's employees. But none remained to see it.